"Did I say which this happens in?" Iris shivered as she stared at the painting. "Maple Ridge or Wolf Branch?"

"No, honey, you didn't," Gena said. "Same with the one with the prison a couple of days ago. I couldn't tell which. But I think you're right. It's one or the other."

"I don't know what to do." Iris paced back and forth, looking at all of the true images, growing stranger and more upsetting as the months passed. "If we go up there with food riots just a few hours away, we might not ever get back. I don't know what the hell the two of us could do about this anyway."

"How long since you've heard from your parents?" Gena caught Iris's hand, then pulled her into a hug.

"The phones have been out for the last couple of weeks." Iris let out her breath in a rush, trying not to cry. "They had it pretty bad over the winter. Trees probably took out the phone lines. Maybe the power lines too."

"That's not what you're dreaming," Gena said. "Nothing as simple as trees. Something's wrong. Those three paintings go together."

"We just have to figure out why."

Into the Storm: Book Three of the Storms of Future Past Series

Copyright © 2019 by Kari A. Kilgore

Published 2019 by Spiral Publishing, Ltd.
www.spiralpublishing.net

Book and cover design copyright © 2019 by Spiral Publishing, Ltd.
Cover art copyright © 2019 by Ig0rzh | Denis Tevekov
|Dreamstime.com

ISBN-13: 978-1-948890-09-0
Library of Congress Control Number: 2018913210

For my uncle, Frank Kilgore

For helping raise awareness of our region as worthy of so much more than extraction and exploitation.

For highlighting the beauty and untapped potential that will carry us and future generations forward, strong and proud.

INTO THE STORM

BOOK THREE OF THE STORMS OF FUTURE
PAST SERIES

KARI KILGORE

SPIRAL PUBLISHING, LTD.

Chapter 1

Most people were a little bit afraid of Iris Rutherford's paintings. The strange ones, at least. And so many of them were strange.

Her home town of Maple Ridge, Virginia, was a former mining camp that hung on when most of the old company coal and timber towns in Appalachia dried up and blew away. Part of it was the stunning beauty of the mountaintop community. Once clearcut and barren, the steep mountains and deep, blue valleys now held mature oaks, pines, poplars, and of course, several stands of huge old sugar maples.

A few people complained bitterly not long after the turn of the century when soaring white windmills appeared to sprout out of the forest, following the curves of the highest ridge lines. Decades later, agreements with a university to test new designs led to free electricity for the residents.

Broad, three-blade models still dominated, joined by single blade turbines and several with more than a dozen blades contained in an outer circle. But many looked more like sculpture, artwork that happened to supply power. Graceful upright blades in endless curves and variations, whirling in a dizzying ballet, bulky control units hidden among the trees.

Most natives and visitors alike now found the additions to the landscape charming, if not beautiful.

The main road into town twisted and curved, giving attentive drivers breathtaking views of the Blue Ridge Mountains, with the sparkling Grasspe River cutting through the valley far below. Enough people pulled off of the narrow two lane road to take a look that muddy wide spots were a permanent fixture.

The town, and the region, were too remote and isolated for anything as official as a scenic overlook. The few tourists who found Maple Ridge were always enchanted, and their business at the restaurant, craft shop, and convenience store was much appreciated.

Visitors savored and treasured their maple syrup and candy, wishing for just one more taste when it was gone.

The other reason Maple Ridge survived was the fiercely independent - some said stubborn - nature of the few hundred hardy souls who clung to their ancestral homes. The elementary and middle school teachers and administration prided themselves as much on their efforts to get less than one hundred students ready for high school and life down off the mountain as on their traditional old school house. The brick walls had been built to last, over one hundred and fifty years ago.

More of those children returned after their educations than folks from other parts of the state would believe. They returned well-qualified from good colleges and universities, frequently after turning down or taking and later leaving excellent jobs elsewhere.

Many took advantage of the lightning speed Internet

brought through town fifty years ago on the way to a bigger town and worked from home. A few took on the challenging but beautiful commute into nearby Wolf Branch or an hour further on to Hidden Springs.

More than the peace and quiet, the slower pace of life, and the deep fondness for the Grasspe River brought so many people back to Maple Ridge. The natives, and after a while the partners they often brought back with them, found they could not do without the peculiar magic and eccentricity of their home.

Iris Rutherford loved her home town as much as anyone else. But her own peculiar magic made her an outsider in a town full of them.

Everything changed for Iris when she started to draw and paint at age eleven. Seemingly overnight, the shy, quiet child who happily let her older brother and sisters take all the attention found her passion. The art teacher, delighted to see such unusual drive and raw talent, offered to let Iris practice before and after school.

She did both.

She understood the technical aspects of composition, color, and balance immediately. Iris surpassed most of what her young teacher had to offer within a few months. She moved on from typical bowls of fruit, faces, and landscapes to startling, surreal visions that even she didn't quite understand.

Shapes often vaguely human, colors that should have clashed but flowed smoothly under her brush, and wild, thick strokes that followed a pattern no one could define poured forth. The art teacher spoke to Iris's parents, and later to the high school art teacher in Wolf Branch. A student with so much promise must be handled carefully, guided in appropriate and controlled paths.

The high school counselor was the first to realize that

whatever drove Iris to spend so many hours practicing would never be controlled.

After enough stern conversations about disturbing the other students, and the teachers, Iris learned to keep her special paintings - the *true* ones - private. She developed great skill with more acceptable work, and the talk died down. She never stopped painting the wild visions and images, the ones she saw burning in her mind as soon as she opened her eyes many mornings.

Her bedroom walls were lined with those distressing sketches and paintings, the ones she had no choice but to get out of herself. Iris learned of abstract and impressionist art from many decades before. She had high hopes of finding acceptance for her true work in art school.

The first person to understand what Iris painted, to see the meaning and significance even she never did, was Gena Wallace.

Chapter 2

The *Eyes of the Future* art exhibit was meant to introduce incoming Appalachian Art Institute students to the community, and let the art-loving residents of Hidden Springs discover up-and-coming talent before anyone else.

The most exciting aspect for Iris was choosing three of her true paintings to go along with the six her teachers suggested.

Other students and even the faculty warned Iris she'd likely be bored to tears and not sell a thing. She was pleasantly surprised to sell everything except the true paintings. She wasn't surprised people barely glanced at those. Not one person asked about them until a soft, rich voice spoke from behind her.

"It's a real shame these aren't for sale."

A small woman stood in front of a large canvas, one Iris had only painted a few days before. She wore typical student garb. Faded blue jeans, brown hiking boots, and a hunter green sweatshirt from the law school in Bountyfield, a couple of hours away. Dark blonde hair hung in a thick braid down her back.

"They *are* for sale," Iris said, standing. She was a few inches taller than the mysterious woman, and at once self-conscious about how much her own black hair provided an unruly contrast. "No one's interested in them, though. They're not as good."

When the woman turned, Iris smiled despite her desire to play the cool, unconcerned artist. She was beautiful, with light brown eyes and full lips curved in a mischievous smile of her own.

"You're mistaken there. The others are nice enough," she said, then a delightful blush spread across her cheeks. "I don't mean that the way it sounds. They're technically just fine. But these are *amazing*. Is this one your family?"

Iris frowned, examining the painting. The background was broad strokes of various shades of green, the swirling patterns overlapping and contrasting. Four distinct oval areas in the middle were black, red, brown, and yellow. Several smaller splashes of the same colors ranged throughout the canvas.

She hadn't named that one. She hardly ever named the true paintings.

Family settled into place in her belly, warm and comforting like hot soup on a cold day.

"I hadn't thought of it that way," Iris said. "Why did you say that? What do you see?"

"Well, I think it's obvious." She pointed to the larger colors. "These are the parents, or adults who go together somehow. The smaller ones are the children. Is that not right?"

Iris shrugged, shaking her head. That was a lie, though. She had no idea where the colors might come from, but every single brush stroke finally made sense. She'd never imagined such a huge group of people all around her, but Iris felt that desire in every part of her now.

"Almost everyone in my family has black or gray hair, so I don't think it's them. Feels right somehow, though."

"Your future family, then. I'm Gena Wallace." Gena turned back to the paintings. "The more I think about it, buying these doesn't seem right. They're pretty personal, aren't they?"

"Iris Rutherford, but I guess you see that on the name card." Iris fussed with the white tag pinned to her shirt, not used to feeling so flustered and awkward talking about her art. In that area if nowhere else, she was normally confident. "I don't know if they're personal, but hardly anyone ever wants to talk about them."

"I think they're the only ones in this whole place worth talking about. What about this one?"

The smaller canvas, only two feet square, disturbed Iris more than she cared to admit. The background ranged from dark red to bright orange. The effect was close enough to flames and blood that even Iris thought it should be warm to the touch. Dozens of gray slashes, many dug deeply into the thick colors underneath, seemed to spill from the middle of the top of the painting all the way to the edges.

"No idea," Iris said, rubbing her upper arms. "Makes me a little anxious even though I painted it."

"Of course it does," Gena said, turning back to the painting and nodding. "If it were bigger, there'd be thousands of dead bodies. Maybe millions. All coming right toward you."

Iris gasped and stepped closer. Her fingers brushed against Gena's arm, but neither of them moved away. That word, *dead*, dropped like a ball of ice through her middle. It was no less true than *family*. She wanted to avoid the unknown slaughter more than she wanted to be part of that family.

Iris knew in her gut the slaughter was coming anyway.

"How are you doing that?" she said, looking into Gena's lovely brown eyes. "I don't even know what they mean. I just wake up with them in my head and I have to get them out."

"I don't know, seems obvious to me. Listen, why don't you mark them as sold. We can work out the price over dinner if you want."

Iris knew, in a flash of understanding as clear as any of the visions she woke up with, that Gena would understand a lot more than her paintings.

Chapter 3

Dinner with Gena led to a date, then another. Before autumn turned into winter, they were spending weekends together at one apartment or the other. None of the boys or girls Iris had dated in high school were worth the trouble after a couple of months. Now hours spent driving didn't frustrate Iris nearly as much as time spent apart.

That frustration led to her first painting that passed into reality.

Iris woke early on the Sunday morning of the first heavy snow in December. Getting out of her bed, away from Gena's warmth and sweet-smelling hair spreading across the pillows, was the last thing Iris wanted.

But the visions never let her sleep in.

She kissed Gena's cheek, then got dressed as quietly as she could. Iris had gotten into the habit of keeping her cleanest painting clothes by the door for days like this. If she finished quickly enough, she might be able to sneak back into bed before Gena was awake.

The apartment's second bedroom, with hardly any space and far too much morning light to be a good place to sleep, was perfect for a miniature studio. Iris kept as much as she could ready in advance, so she could start the coffee then pick up a brush. A sketchpad and colored pencils were a workable substitute at Gena's place.

Several inches of snow turned up the light in the already bright room, shifting it far toward cool blue. That suited the image nearly blinding Iris's mind. Her thoughts wandered as she worked. Her early morning painting was as automatic as the coffee maker.

Even with the tiny electric car on hands-free for the drive between Hidden Springs and Bountyfield, letting Iris read or study or even sleep, the time away from Gena was driving her crazy. And the loneliness she'd felt around her edges for most of her life was far deeper and stronger now that she had someone she missed so badly. Gena had two and a half more years of law school, Iris three and a half of art school.

Something had to change.

Before she'd finished her second cup of coffee and just as she finished the painting, Gena slipped her arms around Iris's waist.

"That's lovely," she whispered. "Perfect for our first house together. You dreamed about that last night, too."

Iris turned in Gena's arms.

"I don't remember any dreams. I hardly ever do."

"You dream all the time," Gena said. She kissed Iris's cheek, then poured herself a cup of coffee. "It's the ones you talk about that show up in your paintings, though."

"You never told me I talk in my sleep."

"I only noticed it a couple of weeks ago." Gena sat on the worn and faded red loveseat, curling her legs beneath her. "We're not sleeping together nearly enough, or I might have caught it sooner."

"What did I say?" Iris said, sitting beside Gena. "We need to find a house?"

"No, nothing that concrete. It didn't make sense until I saw the painting. You said things like 'It's blue,' 'Three of them,' and 'Thirty-seven miles.'" Gena leaned forward with a coffee-scented kiss. "I say there's no reason to get out in this lovely snow anyway. If we're lucky, we won't be able to get out tomorrow. Let's get online and find that house."

THEY MOVED IN TOGETHER before the holidays. The house was indeed blue, with three bedrooms, and thirty-seven miles from Bountyfield. Almost perfectly in the middle of their two schools. Thick trees and seclusion, hidden at the end of the road in a narrow valley, reminded Iris of the best parts of living in Maple Ridge.

Iris did well in her classes, gaining skill in conventional subjects and techniques. The far more important work never left that cozy little house. Sleeping beside Gena turned up the frequency on the visions Iris often worked with, or perhaps cleared out the channel. Either way, her true paintings increased in depth and frequency.

Not all of the paintings, or the dreams, were so positive.

Joyful and happy images continued to appear, but as time passed, the tone turned darker. Gena understood more of each distressing image, and Iris felt the unease of the dreams even though she rarely remembered them.

The world around them reflected the images within.

Food shortages unheard of since the pollinator crisis of the Twenties threatened, then materialized the next winter. Their corner of far southwestern Virginia escaped the riots and starvation, but no one escaped the worry.

Before another year passed, disease joined hunger in Iris's nightmares, on canvas and in her sleep. Turmoil increased in the outside world as well. Death tolls rose to the millions in the US, billions worldwide, as much from violence as hunger and illness. By the time both the law school and the art institute suspended operations in the fall, with the hopes of resuming when things calmed down, neither Iris nor Gena expected they'd ever be graduating.

Along with most people on a planet with a fatally broken food chain, their only hope for the future was surviving.

Chapter 4

Iris paced in front of a huge canvas covered with what looked like several inverted tornados, black and gray and bruised purple. The perspective was strange, with the largest one also the closest, just to the left of center. She not only couldn't remember the dream, this time she barely remembered picking up her brush.

"Did I say which this happens in?" Iris said, shivering as she stared at the painting. "Maple Ridge or Wolf Branch?"

"No, honey, you didn't. Same with the one with the prison a couple of days ago. I couldn't tell which. But I think you're right. It's one or the other."

That prison painting had clusters of dots ranging from a dozen in palest white, more in shades of pink, and a handful in a vivid crimson. Those seemed to glow against the brooding background.

"I don't know what to do," Iris said. She paced back and forth, looking at all of the true images, growing stranger and more upsetting as the months passed. "If we go up there with food riots just a few hours away, we might not ever get back. I don't know what the hell the two of us could do about this anyway."

"How long since you've heard from your parents?" Gena caught Iris's hand, then pulled her into a hug.

"The phones have been out for the last couple of weeks," Iris said. She let out her breath in a rush, trying not to cry. "They had it pretty bad over the winter. Trees probably took out the phone lines. Maybe the power lines too."

"That's not what you're dreaming. Nothing as simple as trees. Something's wrong. Those three paintings go together."

"We just have to figure out why," Iris said. "Sounds simple enough."

She stood in front of the first one she'd done just over a week ago. Most of the canvas was dark orange, with streaks and spots of red and yellow cutting through it. The motion of the brush and the way the colors mixed created a feeling of velocity, of movement. Iris didn't need Gena's remarkable insight to know time was running out on whatever was heading toward them.

"What do you see here now?" she said. "Any different after the one from this morning?"

Gena stood beside Iris with her arm around her waist. They might have been enjoying an art exhibit in some exotic city if the air in her lungs wasn't thick with dread.

"It *is* different. This is a change, a huge transition. Whatever happens here, or doesn't happen, is going to affect everything else. You've heard the gloom and doom news reports about all of us dying out before someone figures out how to stop that disease from the corn?"

"I have," Iris whispered. "They say the tipping point may have already passed."

"This convergence or explosion or whatever it is feels like *it* will be the tipping point. For everyone."

Iris groaned, trying to turn away, but Gena locked her fingers together around her waist. This was too much, for her or anyone else to handle.

"No, don't run away. Tell me what you see here, Iris. What you *feel*."

"I feel like we can't do a damn thing about that one," she said, jerking her chin at the orange painting. "We will all live or die according to what happens there, but we can't make it better or worse. What the hell was the point, then?"

"No, hang on," Gena said. "Look at them together. That and the one from this morning. Look at the colors."

Iris closed her eyes, resisting the urge to slip out of Gena's grasp and walk away. Her unwillingness to deal with her own dreams and visions certainly didn't give her any right to be so rude to her lover. Especially not when Gena was usually right. She opened her eyes, deliberately not focusing on either.

Iris blinked and drew back.

"The red spots," she said, stepping closer. Iris was glad Gena moved with her. "They're the same. Aren't they?"

She moved forward and picked up the orange canvas at the same time Gena picked up the purple and black one. They put them on a double easel they'd made months ago, back when art shows were still possible there or anywhere else in the world.

The dark red spots in both paintings matched perfectly.

"You're right, Gena. They do go together."

"This is something we have to do," Gena said. "Don't you feel that? I don't know what or where, but we can't just ignore this."

Iris's dreams brought the answer that night.

Chapter 5

THE ROOM and the window across from the bed were still dark when Iris woke. The clock was dark, too, yet another power outage. She sat up, trying her best not to wake Gena, but she felt a hand on her shoulder.

"You know, don't you?"

"Did I say something?" Iris said, snuggling with Gena again.

"Yeah. 'We have to go,' over and over again. I still don't know which town, but I feel it in my gut. We can't stay here any longer."

"I'm sorry, Gena. About waking you, dragging you into this craziness, not making any sense half the time. You don't have to go up on that damned mountain with me, you know. Your brother's place in Hidden Springs has plenty of room, and he'd be glad to have you with him."

Gena laughed, the low, throaty sound of it stirring up heat through Iris's body despite her nervousness.

"I'm not going anywhere you're not," Gena said. She kissed Iris, hard and deep. Her warm mouth was almost enough to keep Iris in bed instead of stumbling through the darkness into a cold studio. Almost.

"You do know where we're going. You just haven't caught it yet."

"I know where…" Iris said, her mind fogged with sleep and lust. "Up on that mountain. Come on, gorgeous. Look at something with me."

Each of them grabbed a flashlight, and Iris headed into the studio. The sky was brightening from indigo to pale pink, but it wasn't nearly bright enough to see by yet.

"Can you get the orange one, please?" Iris said as she picked up the purple and black painting. "This will be easier than taking the other one down."

"You mean *Family*, don't you?"

One of the few paintings they'd framed properly hung over the sofa. The shades of green coordinated with the burgundy fabric as if they were made for each other. Iris put her smaller canvas on the cushions, and Gena did the same.

"Just like you said yesterday," Iris said, aiming her flashlight. "Look at the colors."

Gena moved her own beam between the three paintings, not saying anything for several seconds. Iris knew she'd seen it when she grabbed her hand, squeezing tight.

"They match," Gena whispered. "They all match."

Iris stepped forward and picked up the orange painting. She rotated it clockwise until the placement of the red spots matched the red in the larger one. Another turn, and those matched the black spots in *Family*. The same worked for the brown and the yellow markings. She'd never noticed her repetitive pattern in that original painting.

"I don't suppose it's any more strange than you painting this house before we ever saw it," Gena said. "But what the hell is going on here?"

"Whatever we have to do in Maple Ridge goes along with the rest. One leads to the other, I think."

"Or one makes the other possible," Gena said.

As always, her words caught the chaos in Iris's mind, transforming it into harmony.

"For us and everyone else. I don't have a clue what we're supposed to do, though."

"Well, you did say you haven't heard from your family up there," Gena said. "We pack up all this food we've been stockpiling, and whatever else will fit in your big art show van. Then we go up there and see what else falls into place."

"I hope you're right. We could be driving right into a waking nightmare."

Chapter 6

Iris wasn't quite sure if her suggestion was based on a real feeling from her dreams, or from a need to put off the drive up the mountain. Gena either agreed or she was just as nervous. They set the van to drive through Wolf Branch on the way to Maple Ridge, telling themselves it was to make sure that wasn't their destination.

The four lane road through rolling farm country crested a ridge, then followed a wide, gentle curve down toward the Grasspe River. As the van came out of the shadow of a deep road cut, Wolf Branch opened up all around them. The town was as beautiful as ever, even with trees barren for winter.

Tucked into the bend of the river, the small grid of streets followed the gradual rise away from the banks. More buildings and houses followed the contour of the mountains that surrounded downtown, with Iris's high school at one end and the small hospital at the other. No one seemed to be on the streets today.

Several mountains rose up all around, creating a sheltered bowl for the community that felt almost as much like home as Maple Ridge did.

"You should see it in the spring and fall," Iris said as the van slowed, turning right and heading into town. "I'm sorry I never brought you over here for that."

"I'm not so sure we won't be back here, Iris. Don't you feel that?"

Iris glanced at Gena. She had one hand on her chest, gazing out at the neat rows of brick buildings. The pull in Iris's mind, and in her body, was strong to stay right there and not continue on to Maple Ridge. It didn't feel like fear, not really.

This felt like comfort. Like home.

"I do feel it," Iris said. "A pressure in my chest. A good one, like right before I met you."

Gena snorted, but she was smiling.

"That's your high school?"

The three story dark red brick building sat at the highest point on the east end of town, with two matching smaller buildings on either side. A huge flat area off to the side held the football, baseball, and softball fields, with everything painted the same purple and gold Iris remembered so fondly.

A low, white building with *Wolf Branch Cannery* freshly painted in matching purple sat across the high school parking lot. The whole area was much cleaner and more inviting than Iris remembered, with a huge garden area and a greenhouse beside it. Rows of greens, hardy long past frost and snow, still waited for harvest.

"That's it," Iris said. "Everything looks the same, but I don't remember that garden by the cannery."

"A cannery? You mean like canning food?"

"Yeah, they used to be everywhere. This one was open before I went to school here. I remember my grandmother driving down here to can deer meat years ago. Looks like someone is smart enough to have it running again."

Gena wrinkled her nose. "Did you say deer meat?"

"I sure did, smart ass. You wouldn't be a snob about it if you tasted the stew she made in the middle of the winter. There were more deer up there than people, anyway."

"That's probably true most places now, about the deer," Gena said. "No one can be a food snob anymore."

Iris hated to hear that gloomy edge in her voice. Movement caught her eye a few streets away. People were streaming out of the Episcopal church by the time they passed by, the women's dresses and everyone's smiles too bright for a funeral.

"I think we may have crashed a wedding," Iris said.

"Wow. People in Wolf Branch are more optimistic about the future than I am lately."

"Maybe we can do something about that." She took Gena's hand, glancing in the rearview mirror. She never spotted a typical huge white wedding dress, but that many happy people in the middle of the week couldn't be anything else. "Then maybe it will be our turn."

"If we get off of your mountain alive, I'll hold you to that."

Chapter 7

THE VIEWS on the drive up to Maple Ridge were as stunning as ever, maybe even more so. But the feeling couldn't have been more different to Iris. The pressure in her body shifted lower, from warm and comforting to hot and threatening, more so with every twist in the narrow road.

Iris had to disable the autonav so she could drive around many of the potholes, and increasing elevation had her slowing to maneuver through cracks all the way across the faded asphalt.

"Has the road ever been this bad before?" Gena said, holding on to the door as the van rocked over another massive rut. "Looks like it's about to fall off the mountain."

"I've never seen it like this," Iris said. She kept forcing her hands to relax on the wheel, but her shoulders and jaw wouldn't obey her. "Winter's barely started. This has to be from last year and never repaired."

"I'm sorry we didn't get up here more often. We might have seen some of this coming."

"That's not your doing, Gena, don't apologize." She tried her best to keep disgust with herself for not visiting since the previous holidays out of her voice. "We've both been pretty damn busy over the last couple of years. No one besides my parents has made the effort to visit us, either."

The last switchback should have brought only the straight road heading into town into view, with the ever changing models of wind turbines snaking through the ridges. Or at least they had been changing, when people had time and resources enough for testing new designs.

Iris slowed the van to a near stop when she saw a man and a woman standing on either side of the road. Both wore brown scarves that covered most of their faces and carried what looked like old assault rifles.

"What the hell is going up here?" Gena said, gripping Iris's arm.

"Try to look calm. They've already seen us."

The woman spoke into some kind of radio, then walked toward the van. Iris tried to keep her own breath under control as she drove forward. She stopped and rolled her window down an inch when the woman held up her hand. The fierce wind that always blew across the ridge carried the strong odor of menthol cigarettes into Iris's face.

"Some kind of trouble?" Iris said.

"Up to you," the woman said. The rifle was slung over her chest, but she kept her fingers loosely over the trigger guard. "What business you got up here?"

"I grew up here. Haven't been able to reach my family for a couple of weeks. Figured it was time to come check on them."

"Phones down just about everywhere, I guess." She leaned forward and stared at Gena, then looked back at Iris. "Who you up here to see?"

"My parents. I'm not sure why I have to announce myself to get back to my own house."

"Things change here like everywhere when the world goes to hell. Doing what we can to keep Maple Ridge safe. Who'd you say your folks are?"

Iris glanced at Gena, horrified that she'd brought her into whatever this mess turned out to be. Gena should be safe and warm at her brother's house in Hidden Springs. Not facing down fucking assault rifles on a ridge in the middle of nowhere.

"I *didn't* say. Listen, we can head right back down the mountain, no trouble at all. We didn't come up here to cause problems."

The man walked slowly toward them, scarf pulled down to his neck, hand on his own rifle. Iris recognized him from high school when she saw his spiky brown hair and smug asshole grin. Matt…something. A few years older than her, constantly in trouble here, down in Wolf Branch, even as far away as Hidden Springs. Fighting, drinking, assault, even stealing. The dread in her gut sank deeper, threatening to drag her down through the seat.

The woman shook her head. "Well, won't be a problem unless you try to turn this thing around. Tell me who you're here to see. I'll let 'em know you're coming. You two don't much look like thieves. Never can tell these days."

The man, Matt, stopped outside the passenger window. He didn't move, but he didn't take his eyes off Gena, either. His grin deepened into a leer. That was enough.

"I'm here to see Carol and Sid Rutherford," Iris said. "They've lived here their whole lives, just like the rest of my family going back a couple hundred years."

"Thought you might be Iris," the woman said, nodding. Iris still couldn't recognize her face behind that scarf. "Ain't seen you around much since you graduated high school."

"Yeah, I've been real busy. Sure would like to know your name since I can't see your face."

The woman stared at Iris for several seconds, then nodded at Matt. He walked back toward town.

"Suppose you can find out easy enough. Name's Haga. Couple of years behind you in school. We'll make sure your folks know you're on the way."

"I'd appreciate that," Iris said. "We'll see you on the way back out."

"Sure you will."

She stepped back and gestured toward town with the gun. Iris managed not to stomp the accelerator pedal with her shaking legs.

"What the hell," Gena said, her voice just as shaky. "Did she say her name was Haga?"

Iris watched the rear view mirror for several seconds, until she couldn't see those damned rifles anymore. Where did they even get those things?

"Yeah, she always was an odd duck. Her name is Hanna Garrett, but I remember that Haga stuff from years ago. I'd like to know who thought it was a good idea to give her a gun. That guy Matt is a thousand times worse, staring at you like that. I should have left you at your brother's house whether you wanted me to or not."

"What, so you could disappear up here and I'd never hear from you again? I'm harder to get rid of than that."

The road curved to the right, passing through a stand of huge sugar maple trees. Several rows of brick or white clapboard houses lay just beyond. Maple Ridge was every bit as deserted as Wolf Branch, but Iris didn't think for a second people were gathered out of sight for something as positive as a wedding.

"Something's wrong here," she said under her breath.

The street wasn't as damaged as the road into town, but

leaves and debris were piled up along the gutters and drifting across. The usually neat yards in front of the small houses didn't look any better, with branches on the tall grass and several windows boarded up. Iris would have thought it was just another dead logging town.

If there were any reason to have armed guards in front of one.

"What do you feel here, hon?" Gena said. "I can't say I'm feeling a warm welcome."

"I'm feeling like we should keep driving straight through and get out of here. I doubt they left the back road open after all that nonsense."

She turned off a Main Street with rows of shops that looked every bit as abandoned as the houses. Just behind the shops, the two-story Craftsman homes built for long-ago timber barons still stood. The broad lawns and deep porches were in a little better shape, but Iris had never seen her street looking so shabby and abandoned.

She'd also never seen a man carrying another of the old military rifles walking out of her parents' house.

"Stay in the van," Iris said, shutting down the engine.

"Like hell I will. You forget I'm a grown-ass woman, Iris, four years older than you. You go out there, I'm going with you."

Much as she wanted to argue, that tone told Iris it was useless. She got out and activated the security system as the man drew even with her.

No, not a man. Dale Hileman had been a couple of years behind Iris in school, so he was barely seventeen. He smirked as he walked by.

"Come on," she whispered, grabbing Gena's hand. "It's not safe out here."

Dale whistled as he strolled down the street, as if he were walking in a park in the middle of July with a picnic basket. The door opened as soon as Iris stepped onto the porch.

"Get inside," her father said in a low voice. He locked the door, then hugged Iris hard enough to make her spine crackle, then did the same to Gena. His black hair had gone mostly gray in the months since Iris had seen him. "I'm glad to know you're safe, but I wish you hadn't come here."

"What's going on out there, Dad?" Iris said. "People everywhere with guns?"

"Come on through, your mother will want to see you. I wish we could offer you something to eat."

"We brought a bunch of food with us," Gena said.

Iris's father stopped in his tracks, then slowly turned. Lines ran deep into his face, and his shirt was too loose on his frame.

"In your van? We can't leave it out there. It won't last ten minutes. Bring it around to the back yard. At least we can lock the gate and get everything inside."

Iris grabbed his arm as he headed back toward the front door.

"No, wait! Please tell me what's happening. Where's Mom?"

"Nothing that's not going on all over the world, Iris," he said, his voice shaking. "A few assholes have managed to put their own special redneck twist on it up here. With the way people are talking, no women are out on the streets unless they're part of the Asshole Squad. Your mother went down to the den in the basement when that kid knocked on the door."

"Then let's load you and Mom up and get the hell out of here," Iris said. She knew it was already too late for that, and had been from the second Haga saw the van. But she had to try. "Can we get out the back road?"

He shook his head, looking down. In that moment, he looked a hundred years old instead of in his fifties.

"They have a couple of their guards back there. I'm not sure why, though. They blew part of the road off the mountain a couple of weeks ago." He started toward the door again. "I'll tell you everything, what I know at least. But we have to get your van off the street."

Iris followed, tears blurring her vision. How could no one know about this? How could she not have known? She *had* brought Gena into the middle of hell.

"Where did they get explosives that strong?" Gena said as he stopped long enough to check the street before they went outside.

"Word is someone found a stash hidden in a cave not far from here," he said, walking out onto the porch. "Some lunatic must have raided all the mines as they closed down, roadwork jobs, even the armory over in Walton's Gap. They're smart enough to know how to use that old stuff and crazy enough to do it."

"But why force everyone to stay up here?" Iris used her touchkey to open the doors, not trusting her fingers to work the code. Her father's nervousness was seeping into her. "It won't last forever, but there's more food around here than most places in the US. Just not in Maple Ridge."

"They're not after food, not yet. Pull around the block, then go down the alley. They're trying to set up some kind of prison camp here, take charge and scare everyone. I get the feeling they'll steal food before they try to grow it. Steal people, too."

Iris gripped the steering wheel, her already aching hands protesting. She'd heard the family legends just like everyone else, about how the Rutherfords knew more than they should. Other people in Maple Ridge supposedly did, but not as much as her folks.

Asking her father so bluntly, so openly, still made her anxious.

"You get the *feeling* about all of this, Dad?" Iris said. "Or you've been dreaming about it?"

He didn't say anything until after he got out and opened the gate in the chain link fence behind the house. Gena gripped Iris's knee as she drove through.

"It's okay, hon," she said in a low voice. "I think you're on the right track."

Her father looked both sad and proud when he joined them by the back door.

"I always wondered if you'd inherited that," he said. He put his arm around her shoulders for a few seconds, then unlocked the back door of the house. "None of your cousins seemed to. Seemed strange that it would skip a whole generation."

"I didn't know until Gena told me about it," Iris said. Her head swam with both relief and curiosity. "That's what I've been painting all these years. The dreams."

"That's what brought you up here?" he said. "A painting?"

"A few of them," Iris said. "I didn't understand what they were, but Gena helped me figure it out. We brought them with us."

He looked from one to the other of them. He smiled, but his eyes were sad.

"Better get them inside too, then. Come on, let's see your Mom first. She'll take me out herself if we keep her waiting much longer."

Chapter 8

Iris's mother opened the basement door before any of them could knock. The den beyond was comfortable enough, with a couple of old couches, a big TV, and previous generations of gaming systems. It was also pitch dark and cold with the electricity out for the first time Iris could remember. The lantern her father carried didn't reach far.

"Carol, you need to keep this door locked unless you know it's me," he said, shaking his head.

She was thinner than usual, too, and the gray roots in her hair made the aging just as unsettling to Iris. She grabbed both young women at the same time in a breathless hug.

"I heard Iris on the stairs," she said when she stepped back. "Y'all kept me waiting long enough. What are you two *doing* here?"

"Iris has been dreaming about Maple Ridge," Gena said. "Or Wolf Branch. Probably both. We brought her paintings, and food."

"Come on back upstairs," Iris's father said. "We'll bring

everything in, then you need to look at the paintings. See what they tell you."

The curtains were closed in the huge windows in the front of the house, something else Iris had hardly ever seen. A few oil lamps and flashlights made it bright enough to see the paintings.

"How can the power be out? Gena and I saw the turbines turning like usual on the way here."

"That's a fine question, isn't it?" Iris's mother said, scowling. "From what we can tell, the whole town is out. Except for the houses where the people with machine guns live, and their asshole fearless leaders."

"We're not sure about that yet, Carol." Iris's father hunched and relaxed his shoulders, so much smaller than Iris remembered. "But rumor is they're cutting power to Wolf Branch, too, but not all the time like here. Not sure why."

Gena and Iris sat close together on a beige loveseat near the roaring fireplace, trying to stay warm. Iris's mother paced back and forth in front of the paintings, very much like Iris herself often did.

"Something about this one," she said, stopping in front of the orange painting. "It's terrifying. But I'm not afraid of it."

"I was scared," Iris said. "Until we got up here. Something about being here, no matter what's going on, makes that one look a lot less threatening."

"I still don't care for the gray one," Gena said. "They all go together, though."

Iris's mother picked up the gray painting and rotated it, making the colorful spots match like Gena had.

"What did you say this first one was called, Iris?"

"We call if *Family*, but I don't know whose it will be yet."

"The two of you, I'd imagine," her father said. He didn't sound happy. "I think that would be wonderful if things were better. But we'll have to be careful with you here now."

"They're not actually saying that." Gena's face was pale.

"They're paying real close attention to the young women," Iris's mother said. "All the ones that are old enough, or not too old."

"There's not enough food here now," Iris said. She was too sick at her stomach at the thought to imagine eating anything. "What makes them think they'll need breeding stock?"

"I know," her mother said. "You remember Bill Hicks, used to run the convenience store here? And the sugar barn?"

"I remember he was a damn thief," Iris said, taking Gena's hand. "Charged what he wanted when people had no other choice. Anytime there was a blizzard, his prices jumped up until the snow melted."

"Well, he's put himself in charge of everything up here," her father said. "Even rounded up everyone's hunting dogs, says he'll make sure they're fed and trained up *properly*. A lot like what he's trying to do to the humans. Most of us think Rita Hicks is helping run the show, but he's the one running his mouth."

"They're planning to raid somewhere close by for food," her mother said. "Probably Wolf Branch, but we're not sure. Between that and hunting with all those dogs, he figures he'll have enough to need the young women before much longer."

"He's just proclaiming this?" Gena said. "Not even trying to hide it?"

"Not in so many words, no," Iris's father said. He added another log to the fire, then sat on the couch beside the paintings, hands dangling between his knees. "Mostly a lot of talk about getting us all through this crisis that the outside world can't handle without a bunch of riots and killing."

"He hasn't killed anyone yet," her mother said. "Not that we know of. But no one doubts that he will."

They all jumped when someone knocked at the door. The pounding was hard enough to rattle the windows.

"Downstairs," Iris's father said, jumping to his feet. "All of you, go."

"I'm sorry we're causing so much trouble," Iris said, "but they know we're here. Won't hiding make it worse for you?"

"Come on, Sid." Her mother held out her hand. "She's right. I'm sick of hiding anyway."

He scowled, but he didn't argue. He did hold his arm out to keep everyone else behind him when he opened the door.

Haga stood on the porch, still carrying her rifle slung across her back. She'd pulled the brown scarf around her neck. The awkward school girl with acne and limp hair was long gone, a beautiful young woman taking her place. Haga's dark brown hair gleamed, and her skin was pale and flawless. The slight smile curving her full lips said she was fully aware of her transformation and how it affected others.

She showed no sign of the hungry gaunt look over-taking Iris's parents.

"Glad to see you're settling in," Haga said, nodding. "Want you to feel right at home."

"We were planning to take Mom and Dad down to Hidden Springs for the holidays," Iris said, stepping in front of her father. "We can bring supplies up to you when we come back. Just let us know what you need."

"Well, that sure is a generous offer, Iris. Not sure we'll be able to accommodate you there, but you never know about such things."

Iris's father put both hands on her shoulders, pulling back a tiny bit.

"What do you want, then?" he said. "Come inside out of the cold."

"Mr. Hicks and Mrs. Hicks want to welcome you both personally," Haga said. She made no move to step in and stop the slight heat from escaping. "They remember you fondly, Iris, and they'd like to meet your friend here."

"Maybe another time," Iris's mother said. "These two need a rest from the drive up."

"They've been awful busy, better all around if they come on in now." Haga shifted her arms enough to reveal a handgun in a holster around her waist. "Won't keep you long. We all need our rest for the hard times coming up."

Iris closed her eyes for a second, then looked back at Haga. Orange and red flames rose in a halo behind her shoulders and head, Iris's painting brought to moving, disturbing life. And the motion was pulling inward, not pushing Haga back out into the cold. The same feeling pulled like an anchor attached to Iris's spine.

"That's fine, send them in," she said. Her mother drew breath to speak and her father squeezed her shoulders, but she went on. "If we're going to be here a while, we should get to know folks."

"Just give us a minute?" Iris's mother said. "We can't offer you much, but I'll get something to drink."

"So kind of you." Haga's smile was full and confident this time. "I know they'll appreciate that as much as I do."

She stepped back and let Iris's father close the door. He turned to Iris, his brow drawn down.

"What the hell are you thinking?"

"Wait, just listen," Iris said. "If they're after breeding stock, they're not going to hurt us. Gena, can you please grab that bottle of rum we brought? We'll be as hospitable as we possibly can."

"No, this is ridiculous," Iris's mother said. She peeked out the living room window. "Bill in his damned SUV, uses up what little gas we can get anymore. What good can this possibly do?"

"I saw something," Iris said, trying to find the words. She took the bottle and glasses from Gena and arranged them on the coffee table. "Just now, flames raging all around her head. This has something to do with that orange painting. You saw as clear as we did that that one is important."

"You saw it, like a vision?" her father said.

"Right behind her, clear as I see you right now." Iris said. "That never happened to me before."

Her father stared into her eyes for several seconds, apparently finding what he needed to see. He gathered up all the paintings and hid them behind the couch.

"Sit with me," he said stepping over to the door. "Don't let them get between us."

Chapter 9

BILL HICKS HAD LOST ALL of the dark brown in his thick, spiky hair since Iris had last seen him, but he was still every bit as intimidating. He'd grown a thick gray mustache to match, and he towered over her father.

Rita Hicks could easily be mistaken for someone's kindly youngish grandmother, with her blond-streaked-with-gray hair pulled back in a sensible ponytail. She was almost six feet tall herself, and her figure was soft and matronly. That softness did not extend to her pale gray eyes.

"You remember Iris," Haga said, closing the door behind her. "I didn't catch her friend's name."

"I didn't give it," Iris said. She sat on the couch between her mother and Gena, with her father sitting on the arm.

"I'm Gena Wallace."

"I'm certainly glad to see you again, Iris, and to meet you, Gena," Mr. Hicks said. He and his wife sat on the loveseat close to the fire. Neither of them removed their heavy denim coats. "What a pleasant surprise in the middle of difficult times to see both of you up here."

Haga stood by the door, her guns too visible to forget. Iris didn't want her parents any more involved than they already were.

"I'll be honest," Iris said. "We came up here to bring my parents back to our place. Looks like they're not getting enough to eat."

"Well, that's been a problem, with such trouble out in the world," Mrs. Hicks said. Neither she nor her husband looked like they'd missed a meal. "That won't be a problem much longer."

"Then you don't mind if we make it a little bit easier," Iris said. "Give you four less mouths to feed."

Mrs. Hicks leaned forward and picked up the bottle of rum. She filled the seven small glasses with a half-smile.

"Seems like you're pretty direct, just like when you were in school," she said, pushing a glass toward Iris. "So I'll do the same. We'll have plenty to eat and a safe place to raise new little mouths. You two are perfect for that."

Iris tossed the tall shot back. The rum was cold and burning, but she managed to keep a straight face. Everyone else picked up their glasses. Both of her parents' hands were shaking.

"You might be missing an important point here," Gena said. She took Iris's hand in her clammy one. "Iris and I are engaged. The battle over telling people who they could and couldn't marry ended forty years ago."

"I don't give a damn about who you marry," Mr. Hicks said. He leaned back and crossed his long legs at the ankles. "No one else does, either."

"See, this isn't a question of anyone's battles." Mrs. Hicks poured herself another full shot. "Some people still carry on about religion and the law, but none of that matters anymore. All that fuss and nonsense is in the past. I'm afraid all you got left now is biology. And that's exactly what you're going to fulfill."

"I think we've heard just about enough," Iris's father said. He leaned forward, but he didn't stand. "No one in this house is interested in your little project, Bill."

"Interested or not doesn't matter anymore, either," Mrs. Hicks said. "In case you haven't noticed, the world is in the process of tearing itself to pieces all around us. I'd wager we'll see more people dead than alive by the end of this winter."

"I dreamed of you coming back home, Iris," Mr. Hicks said.

Cold sweat covered Iris, but she tried her best not to show it. She wondered if these two were among the dead bodies in her paintings.

"Did you now?" she said in a reasonably calm voice.

"You and your friend here," he said. "I didn't know who she was, but the dream was clear as day. I saw the two of you with many healthy children. Those babies will be the salvation of all of us."

Iris clenched her fist until her hand ached. She wished for more of the rum, but she didn't want everyone to see how badly she was shaking.

Those words sounded true to her. They felt true, in her whole body and mind. Gena's trembling against her said she felt the same.

"Well, all this talk and we lost sight of why we dropped by in the first place," Mrs. Hicks said. She had the same broad, perfect smile she used to welcome tourists to their overpriced shops in town. "You must be worn out from that long drive with so much going bad out in the world. Hadn't seen your folks in a while, Iris, been so busy. I think you're right. I'm sorry to say they're looking a bit unwell."

"We brought you all a good supply of food." Mr. Hicks nodded at Haga, then tossed his shot of rum back. "Should be enough for several fine meals for all of you. Wouldn't want anyone to get too thin and unhealthy now that you're safe and sound back home."

Haga lowered her head and smiled at Iris, her eyes sharp as any predator's. She stepped outside for a few seconds, then came back in with Dale Hileman, smug Matt from the guard post on the main road, and one other man Iris didn't recognize. All of them carried boxes filled with food into the kitchen.

And they all had the old machine guns slung over their backs.

"We brought plenty of food for the four of us," Gena said, her voice strong. "Maybe the neighbors could use this instead."

"That's a generous offer," Mrs. Hicks said, standing. "Gena, isn't it? We want to make sure everyone here is safe and healthy."

Her husband stood beside her.

"In fact, we'll leave two of our finest guards here to make sure of it," he said. "Iris, you already know Haga, and I believe you know Dale, too. They'll take the first shift. If you need anything at all, you just let one of them know. They'll take care of it."

"Glad to be of service," Dale said. His smile slipped past leering into predatory. Matt stood shoulder to shoulder with him, grinning before he actually winked at Iris.

"You two get settled in and don't worry about a single thing," Mrs. Hicks said. "We're taking care of everything to make sure Maple Ridge is the safest place in the world for you and all of your children."

Chapter 10

IRIS WALKED from one side of her childhood bedroom to the other, doing her best to avoid the wooden floorboards that squeaked. Nine steps, from the shelf-covered wall that still held many of the books and toys she'd outgrown a decade before to the nearly floor to ceiling windows at the back of the house. She was thankful she'd replaced the frilly little girl purple curtains with sensible blue panels before she moved out.

"Iris, honey, you got to come to bed."

Dim light from an oil lamp on the nightstand showed Gena, already burrowed down in the heavy blankets that matched the curtains. The full-sized mattress was a close but cozy fit for both of them, and her lover's warmth in the frigid house was tempting.

The sharp aftermath of the coffee she'd had too much of with dinner didn't feel like quite enough to keep her awake if she got too comfortable.

Iris switched directions instead, her bare feet numb with the cold. Twelve steps this way, from the bathroom door to the hall door, both still full of tiny holes where she'd hung countless of her smaller paintings over the years. For the first time in her life, Iris wasn't curious about the next thing her mind would create. She was too horrified by what she could already feel coming.

"It's after midnight and I'm freezing to death," Gena said. "There's nothing more either of us can do tonight."

"I know that, Gena. I know. We never should have come up here in the first place."

That was a lie, one Iris wasn't comfortable telling herself anymore. Every part of her knew she was exactly where she was supposed to be, and that Gena was too. That didn't make the danger for everybody in Maple Ridge any easier to take. Or the idea of going to sleep any less terrifying.

"Maybe not, but we *are* here." Gena sat up, clutching the blankets under her chin. "Neither of us will be any damn good tomorrow if we don't get some rest. What's wrong with you?"

Iris stopped beside one of the windows, wishing it weren't too cold to open it. She'd stared out at the trees behind the house for hours as a kid, watching the way they moved together, listening to them whisper to each other. Anything to quiet her whirling mind before she'd known picking up a paint brush would do that. Now bringing the looming vision into reality was the last thing she wanted.

"I'm afraid to go to sleep," she whispered.

"Come here and talk to me about it, then," Gena said. She held out one hand. "You're driving me crazing pacing like that."

"I'm driving *me* crazy too." Iris sat on the bed and took Gena's warm hand. "I don't know what else to do."

"Listen to me. At least come here and keep me warm for a little while. Why are you afraid, sweetheart?"

Gena put both arms around Iris's shoulders. The heat of her body was too much to resist.

"I know what you're trying to do," Iris said.

She slipped under the covers anyway. They both wore thick flannel pajamas scavenged from her father's old clothes.

"Don't you touch me with those ice feet," Gena said, and Iris could hear her smile from the long-standing joke between them. "I'm trying to keep from freezing to death. Now tell me what's going on."

Iris let Gena pull her back against the cushioned purple headboard, a remnant of her middle school decorating scheme that hadn't yet been replaced. Her legs and lower back ached with cold and tension.

"I'm not sure how to say it," she said. "I feel like I'm dreaming already. Like part of my brain is taken over even when my eyes are still open. This is not going to be a good dream."

"Maybe it's just stress." Gena kissed the top of her head. "The last few weeks have been a nightmare. Today certainly was."

"I don't think so. It's more than that." Iris tried to wipe her tears before Gena saw them. "I don't *want* to see what's coming. Not anymore."

The truth was agony had settled into Iris's chest, the worst broken-hearted longing she'd ever experienced. She didn't want to dream of the horrible loss heading toward them, even if she didn't remember when she woke. She wasn't certain she'd survive pain so deep once she knew what was going to cause it.

"Shhhhh, I got you," Gena whispered into her ear. "I'm not going anywhere, no matter what happens."

"You don't know that," Iris said, not bothering to stop

her tears now. "No one feels safe to me. We're in the middle of something terrible here."

"And yet we have to be here, right? We both knew that before we left."

"Yeah, we have to be here. I still feel that. But I don't want to know why anymore."

"I have an idea," Gena said. She scooted down under the covers. "Keep me warm for a little while. See how you feel if you stay still and listen to my heartbeat. I know I'll feel a hell of a lot better than shivering under here by myself."

"For a little while," Iris whispered.

She had every intention of getting back up as soon as Gena fell asleep, maybe even going back downstairs for more of the cheap, bitter coffee the guards brought with them. A few minutes curled up around Gena, face against her breasts, the soothing rhythm of a heartbeat in her ear, left Iris barely able to keep her eyes open. The long, difficult, frightening day and rich, heavy meal settled into her limbs, pulling her under despite her fear. Her sleep was sound and deep.

The dream threatened without coming to life in her mind, or under her brush, that night or the next few.

Iris didn't truly see what was coming until only minutes before the nightmare burst into reality.

Chapter 11

THE ROUTINE WAS the worst part. Every day exactly the same, with no promise or even a threat of change. Bill and Rita Hicks didn't return, but the rotating pair of guards never left, each shift bringing fresh supplies. Iris's mother seethed at the repeated deliveries of food they hadn't seen in town for months, but none of them refused the meals.

Worry about what the cost would turn out to be never left any of them.

Iris's father walked along Main Street at least once every day, usually at dawn, hoping for news from the outside. None of the other local men outside the makeshift militia had heard anything. The fear in his eyes when he begged the three of them to stay inside worked, but Iris wasn't the only one losing patience with virtual imprisonment.

Books, games, even painting failed to distract any of them for more than a few minutes.

Even with her odd senses, and Gena's, telling her they had to stay, Iris's mind twisted and writhed, desperate for a way out. By the end of the week, she was ready to beg for something, anything different.

The long-anticipated and dreaded dream left her wanting to beg for dull routine to return.

Iris opened her eyes in the frigid pre-dawn light, looking right into Gena's. Her lover sat against that absurd headboard, arms wrapped around her knees.

"You know," Gena whispered.

"I don't remember anything. What did I say?"

Gena shook her head.

"What do you see, Iris? A new painting?"

Cold worse than the chilly room moved from Iris's heart out through her body, raising gooseflesh all over.

"No, not a new one." She shivered, but Gena didn't move closer. "I see the one with the gray tornadoes."

"Same one I see," Gena whispered. "But they're moving now."

Both women jumped at a sharp rap on the door.

"Wake up," Iris's mother said, her voice sharp. "Come on now."

Iris opened the door before she could knock again. Carol Rutherford's hair stood on end and her cheek still held pillow creases. She held a flashlight in one hand and clutched her heavy blue robe tight against her chest with the other.

"Something's going on in town," she said, glancing over her shoulder. Iris could hear her father moving around downstairs. "They're rounding women and children up. Your Dad heard they're taking us to the sugar barn."

"What for?" Gena said. Her grip on Iris's hand was painfully tight.

"Dad heard where they're taking us?" Iris said. "Where are they taking *him*?"

Her mother's face clenched tight for a second, then she shook her head.

"No one knows, or at least they're not saying. He thinks we don't have long, so gather up what you can before the guards come charging in here."

She walked down the hall toward their bedroom, her feet silent in thick wool socks.

"The sugar barn?" Gena said, her teeth chattering. "Where they sell the maple syrup?"

"Yeah, sell it, make it, store it, the works." Iris pushed the door shut. She nearly ran into the bathroom, stepped up onto the toilet, and reached on top of the medicine cabinet. "I used to work weekends helping cook it down, out in the store selling it. Painted a few advertisements for them once I started college."

After a few panicked seconds of fumbling, her fingers brushed against ridged metal. Iris pulled the ring into her hand and stepped down, blowing dust away from two keys.

"I pretended I lost these my last year working in the back," she said. The keys jangled when she dropped them onto her dresser. "I had no idea why at the time. Not sure why I'm getting them now, either."

"Any advantage can't hurt," Gena said. Both women pulled on jeans, t-shirts, and flannel shirts, and Iris tucked the keys into the tiny watch pocket at her hip. "Has your Dad heard what they're planning to do?"

"Not that he's told me." Iris sat on the bed and pulled Gena down beside her. "Listen, you were upset when I woke up. What did I say, Gena? Come on, I need to know what we're walking into here while we can still warn him."

Gena hesitated, staring at the floor before she met Iris's gaze.

"You said something about a grandfather," she said. "Their grandfather."

Iris felt a hollow space in her middle, an odd fit to her lover's words. That was the truth, but maybe not all of it. Before she could say anything, a heavier knock startled her.

"Time to go," her father said.

He wore heavy work pants and a lined winter jacket, and he held leather work gloves. The gauntness was leaving his face after several days of steady meals, but the bruised hollows under his eyes had only gotten worse.

"Same place you're going?" Iris said, watching him closely.

"I don't know. I don't think so. Just dress warm."

Haga and Dale Hileman stood in the living room, both holding their rifles for the first time since Iris and Gena arrived. A sullen glare had replaced Dale's smug grin. Iris saw the swirling flames behind both of them, even stronger than before. She was honestly surprised she couldn't feel the heat in the freezing cold room.

"Move it now," Dale said. "Don't want to keep 'em waiting."

"Who would we be keeping, Dale?" Iris's mother said, coming down the stairs behind them. "I'd like to know where my family is being dragged at the ass crack of dawn. And why the hell we should go with you in the first place."

"You go where I say and when I say," Dale said, his voice rising. "Unless you want to see your daughter and her pretty little friend living up to their biology right here and now!"

Dale lunged forward.

Sid Rutherford pushed Iris and Gena back and stepped in front of his wife.

"That's enough," Haga said. She never moved, and her voice wasn't loud, but Dale froze. "Every one of you settle down."

The younger man stood inches from Iris's father, face

red and fists clenched. Iris smelled strong coffee on his breath, and stronger whiskey.

"I said settle down, Dale." Haga's voice was calm, but Dale stepped back, shaking his head. "These two won't go to the likes of you, and you know it."

"Then what's the damn point?" Dale shoved the front door open hard enough that it slammed against the wall.

"The point is for each and every one of us to do our part so we all have a future," Haga said. She jerked her chin toward the door. "Do your job, and you'll get your reward. We all will. Keep causing trouble, and you'll pay the price."

Iris knew her words were meant for Dale, but Haga stared at her and her family. Dale's rifle was now slung over his back. Haga carried hers over one shoulder. Much easier and faster to reach.

Especially with Haga's calm demeanor, Iris had no doubt which of the two was in charge.

And who would make sure that price was paid.

Chapter 12

THEY WALKED IN SILENCE, the two guards behind them. The feeble winter sun still hadn't risen at nearly seven. Iris recognized other families heading toward the middle of town, each with their own armed escorts. Everyone moving in the same direction, at least for now.

Iris forced her free hand to her side, away from the small bulge in her pocket.

When they turned onto Main Street, Iris saw two groups forming in the distance. Women and children in front of the log-fronted sugar barn, and men beside the brick school building on the other side of a graveled parking lot. Guards surrounded both, but the ones around the men held their rifles in their hands rather than slung over their shoulders.

"Taking volunteers, are you?" her mother said. She held her husband's hand, her knuckles white.

"Call it whatever you want to," Haga said from behind them. "Won't make a damn bit of difference in the end."

A low moan ahead of them caught all of Iris's attention.

A vaguely familiar woman pushed against the guards by the barn, trying to get to two men walking toward the school. The older man put his arm around the younger, keeping him from turning back.

"Sam Williams," Iris's father said under his breath. "And his youngest boy, Ben."

The woman ahead of them, Sam's mother, wailed again. Bill Hicks broke away from the crowd of men, Matt with his grin close behind. Bill held one arm low, out of sight behind his body. Rita Hicks moved from the middle of the women, closer to Mrs. Williams.

"Ben was in school with me." Iris tried to will Ben's mother to be still, be quiet. She didn't want to see how the disruption would be dealt with.

When Ben's mother cried out again, Rita Hicks put her arm around the much smaller woman's shoulders. Iris was close enough to see Mrs. Williams try to pull away.

Bill Hicks reached the two men, speaking too softly for anyone else to hear. Both turned back toward the women. Matt stepped sideways between their little group and the other men. Before anyone else could move, Bill swung a short iron pipe.

Iris did hear the sickening thump as it connected with the side of the young man's knee.

Mrs. Williams' scream drowned out her son's, but Rita Hicks held her firm, not letting her move forward or look away. Both crowds shuffled, but no one broke out of the loose circles.

"Why aren't they fighting back?" Gena whispered. Her hand was a vise on Iris's arm.

"They're half-starved," Iris's father said. His plodding march never slowed. "More than half terrified. We've had it a lot better than most of them."

Mr. Williams tried to help his son stand, but Ben screamed again as his leg buckled under him. Matt tried to hide his face, but his laugh rang out in the cold air. Mrs. Williams fell to her knees in the dusty parking lot, hands over her mouth.

Rita Hicks crossed her arms and returned her own husband's smile.

"Shame to waste a good man like that," Haga said. Iris could hear the smile in her voice, too. "Might open up the way for Dale here."

"Fuck off, Haga." Dale kept his eyes forward. "You'll end up on your back before all's said and done."

"We'll see about that, I suppose. If I do, won't have a damned thing to do with you."

The violence may not have been specifically for Iris and her family, but it worked. Iris's mother hugged her father tight, fast enough that neither of them stopped walking. She grabbed Iris's hand as she and Gena continued toward the women's side.

"There you go," Haga said, nodding. "Just do what you ought to and this will all go better than you think."

Iris opened her mouth, but sharp pressure on both her hands kept her from speaking.

"Now's not the time," Gena whispered. "Can't you feel it?"

Iris closed her eyes, wishing she could deny the clammy chill in her gut. Right now, they were caught.

Right now, the wrong move could get everyone she loved killed. Or worse.

Right now, all she could do was watch. And wait.

A few more people followed, splitting silently to the men's or women's sides, then the streets were empty along with all the storefronts opposite the school and the sugar barn. Haga and the other women with guns stood in an arc around the women and children. Iris wished Dale didn't stand so close to her father.

Bill Hicks walked away from Ben Williams without a backward glance. Neither Ben, his mother, or his father made a sound now. Rita Hicks joined her husband on the street between the two groups. Matt stood behind them, arms crossed, rifle clearly visible.

"Now listen up," Bill said, his voice sharp and clear. "We're real sorry to drag you out in the cold at such an hour. But we got things we need to take care of. The kind of dangerous work that means we have to split families up for the time being."

Rita stepped forward. Iris wondered if they'd rehearsed this whole speech.

"I know some of you don't like the way things are changing, here and out in the world. You're gonna have to understand that things *have* changed, though. And me and Bill are doing everything we can to make sure we get through these hard times. Each and every one of us has a role to play. Roles as old as time itself."

The men gathered in front of Ben Williams, almost too slowly to see. Iris was torn between fear and pride as her father stepped right in front of him.

Bill Hicks didn't notice, or he pretended not to.

"The safest place we have to keep you women and children is in the sugar barn. We can't protect you out in all your houses, and you're going to need protection. Some of the guards will stay with you, but we can't spare many when we go."

Iris felt her mother start forward. She made it a few steps before Iris and Gena managed to grab her. Carol Rutherford's whole body vibrated.

"Where the hell do they think they're going?" she

nearly growled, still pulling forward. "What kind of madness is this?"

"Madness we're not going to survive if we do this now," Iris said into her mother's ear. "They're all armed. Haga's looking right at you, Mom. Dale hasn't looked away from Dad. We have to wait!"

Rita Hicks took her turn, staring at Iris and Gena.

"Many of you share the same gift of the sight that me and Bill do. Most of us knew hard times were coming. What you might not know is we've been holding off, waiting for the right time to do what we have to do. The last pieces of that vision are in place. We got to act now to protect our future."

Iris was one of the few who didn't jump at the squeal of wood and cold metal behind her. Two men pushed the broad red-painted doors to the sugar barn open, wheeling them back along their tracks. What looked like old traditional wood slats on both sides was actually solid metal with tight weatherproof seals.

Despite the frigid temperatures, the men didn't bother with the smaller single door set off to the side for cold weather days. Dust and stale air cut through the crisp morning.

"Don't worry now," Bill Hicks said. He smiled and held up one hand as if he were comforting a fussy child. "We'll get the heat turned on right quick, and we have plenty to feed you. Your men will be right over at the schoolhouse until it's time."

The two semi-circles of guards didn't say anything. They just started walking forward. Iris willed herself to resist, to stand right where she was. To at least make sure they knew she wasn't going without a nasty fight.

Her father met her gaze across the parking lot. He

shook his head, almost too fast to see, then turned and followed the rest of the men and boys.

Iris didn't have to hear him to understand. She wasn't there to fight. Not yet. She had to keep Gena and her mother safe until they could all get away.

She walked into the sugar barn, still holding her mother and her lover's hands.

Chapter 13

The only thing that had changed in the store right inside the barn doors since Iris last saw it was a thick layer of dust. Shelves made of pine stained brown covered the walls, still piled high with tourist junk. Wooden whistles and flimsy knives, cheap harmonicas, rough-edged cap guns with rolls of red tape for bullets.

Iris's parents told her this stuff was antiquated garbage when her grandparents were alive, already mass produced overseas. But strangers who found their way to Maple Ridge bought handfuls of it. Rotating stands full of postcards, books, and download cards for screechy mountain music dotted the center of the rough-hewn hardwood floor. The gummy filth over everything looked like no one had found their way up here for a long, long time.

The only spaces cleared of dust and everything else were supposed to hold food. Bins for chips and crackers, shelves for bottles of maple syrup and boxes of candy, even the huge wall coolers for soda and water stood empty.

Iris suspected Bill and Rita Hicks had hidden everything edible away rather than selling it to tourists or anyone else. Maybe in the locked production and storage area at the back of this sprawling building. She forced herself not to check her watch pocket for the keys.

At least fifty women and young children had room to move around in the store, but hardly anywhere to sit down. Sunken eyes and bony faces made it clear most hadn't had regular meals for a while, especially the pale, quiet children. Only a few were dressed for winter weather instead of wearing night clothes.

Two women Iris remembered from grade school helped Mrs. Williams sit on the chair behind the long checkout counter, behind the antique cash register no one knew how to use.

Mrs. Williams was silent now, but tears ran down her crumpled, red face.

Haga strolled through the crowd, rifle still over her back, a sneer curving her lips. She nodded to one of the guards still outside. He stepped away for a second, then the long lights overhead popped and buzzed into life. Seemed the power did work where the people in charge wanted it to.

Steam rose from Haga's mouth when she spoke into the clammy air. Iris was sure it was near freezing inside even without the broad doors standing open.

"Don't be shy, now, move whatever you need to out of the way. Not likely we'll need any of this crap for suckers to buy anytime soon. Get yourself comfortable however you need to."

Iris grabbed piles of dark green t-shirts from hangers beside her, wadding them up to hide the image of the sugar barn printed on the front. Her mother and Gena passed them along. That would do fine for sitting on the floor, but not much to keep warm. The pile of blue and red sweatshirts under the shirts wasn't nearly enough for everyone.

"Can we please get the heaters on?" Iris said, handing out the last of the sweatshirts. She raised her voice over the noise of women dragging displays across the floor. "It's freezing in here."

Haga turned slowly, sneer deepening into a smile. She wasn't going to miss one damn chance to show her power to a group she was certain didn't have any.

"Mr. Hicks said he'd get that done, and he will. I'd imagine he's too busy next door to worry about that right now."

"I know how to start them." Iris crossed her arms and met Haga's gaze. "I worked here for years."

"Yeah, a bunch of us did, Iris." Haga shook her head, still smiling. "And like I told you, Mr. Hicks will take care of it."

"Iris…" Gena whispered. Her cold fingers slipped along Iris's wrist to her hand.

The crackling orange flames danced behind Haga again, so clear and bright Iris was surprised no one else saw them. The flames drew Iris forward rather than pushing her away.

"Then at least get us something to eat," Iris said. "None of us had breakfast, and I know the kids are hungry. Have been for a long time, by the looks of them."

"That's awful sweet talk for someone who hasn't much been up here for the past couple of years." Everyone moved aside as Haga walked forward, stopping inches in front of Iris. "Seems to me you got better things to worry about than running your mouth."

Flame blocked everything behind Haga now, turning the whole room into a raging inferno that even *felt* hot to Iris. She smelled the burning, heard fierce crackling and roaring wind.

But she knew without needing to see that all the

women behind the guard were moving, too, standing shoulder to shoulder in front of their children and the oldest among them.

Iris didn't understand the shape of it yet, but she knew Haga, Matt, Bill and Rita Hicks, and everyone else who assumed they were in control of Maple Ridge had badly misunderstood how these desperate people would behave.

After staring up into Iris's eyes for a long moment, Haga stepped back and turned toward the room.

"Now listen here. Best way to get food for your children is to keep yourselves calm. Best way to keep the power for the lights on, too. Best way to sit here cold and hungry in the dark is to think about causing trouble."

Haga grinned at Iris this time before she strode out of the building. Two of the male guards rolled the barn doors closed. Iris was sure they purposely made as much noise as they could chaining and locking them.

A low whisper moved like waves through the store, no one daring to raise their voices. The wall of fire departed with Haga, leaving Iris with a clear view of everyone's eyes. Only a few were avoiding hers. Most met her gaze and nodded.

"What were you playing at, Iris?" Gena said into her ear. "She's got a fucking rifle!"

"I know she does. Everyone else knows, too. That's the whole point."

Iris held up her hands for a few seconds, until every woman looked her way. She whispered into Gena's ear, then her mother's.

"Tell them to keep talking, but not too loud. Move around a little. I'm going to check the security systems."

Gena tried to keep Iris from walking away, grabbing her hands. Iris squeezed them, smiled, and jerked her head toward her mother. Carol Rutherford was whispering to the women nearest her, who then turned to whisper to someone else. The noise level was rising again. Gena scowled and turned away.

Iris moved toward the checkout counter, stopping every few steps to help someone. She wasn't surprised to find the smaller entry door beside the big rolling doors locked tight, the keys in her pocket useless for that.

Her message moved so quickly that Mrs. Williams rolled the chair to the side before Iris got there.

"Let me get out of your way, honey," she said. "You can sit down right here and do whatever you need to do."

"You're fine right where you are." Iris pulled the smaller woman into a quick hug. "I'm so sorry."

"We have got to get out of here, Iris, and make sure they don't get away with what they're trying. Now, what do you need me to do?"

Iris glanced out at the store, a perspective she knew well from summer and winter shifts behind this counter. More than a few times, she'd been resetting or updating the payment systems.

Or the security systems.

If the cameras had started back up after the power was off, the casual but constant movement should be distraction enough for anyone who happened to be watching.

"Just sit tight. The security cameras won't work without the town's internet connection. That's on a different circuit. I'm betting no one thought to start that up or link them together."

Mrs. Williams nodded, dabbing the corners of her eyes with the corner of her scarf.

"They've had the internet shut down for months now, just like the power. Last thing them assholes want is for us to get word to the outside world."

Iris pulled a black metal drawer from under the

counter, then raised a flat glassy display barely the size of both of her hands up. She didn't raise the screen waist high, like anyone standing here helping dozens of customers would. That would be too easy for anyone on the other side of the security cameras to catch.

The screen was dark, definitely a good sign. She pressed her fingertips into a nearly invisible bar on the bottom edge. While she waited for the store's system to start up, Iris thought through all the cameras she knew about.

Not quite as big as her pinky fingernail, the networked devices were scattered anywhere small things might be slipped into a pocket. Above the racks of music download cards, hidden in the shelves that used to hold maple candy.

Iris knew at least a couple were behind her with a good view of the screen that flashed into grey and blue life. Bill Hicks might not understand a whole lot about how the store systems worked, but he was always eager to find someone to yell at.

System Check Failure: Establishing Connection…

Iris puffed air out through her cold lips. That connection wasn't going to get anywhere until - unless - someone outside started up the town's server.

"The whole thing is still offline," she said. "Cameras and everything. That will make the rest a lot easier."

Mrs. Williams touched Iris's arm before she could walk away.

"Make what a lot easier? What if Bill remembers to turn everything else on? I hear he's taking a lot more care with all our poor dogs than he is with any of us. Saw that for myself a little while ago, too."

Iris didn't have to hear her unspoken question.

What if they hit you like they did my boy?

Or your mother?

Or Gena?

"Bill won't, not likely, anyway. He's plenty good at running things in the back and yelling at everyone out here. Not so much at this part. We'll have to watch out for Rita, though."

Iris walked toward the back of the store, waving for Gena and her mother to join her. The heavy steel double doors were painted to match the rustic plank siding everywhere else. If Bill hadn't changed the locks or chained this door like the one at the front, they might still have a chance of fighting back.

"What did you find?" Gena said, grabbing Iris's hand.

"Cutting the power cut the internet," Iris said. "For the store and most of the town. I'm sure Bill and Rita had no such problems at their house. But for now, no one's remembered to restart the security cameras."

The three women stood shoulder to shoulder, with Iris in the middle. She fit the key into the doorknob, holding her breath until it slipped into place.

"But one of them could remember to turn the damn thing on," her mother said. "Any second now. Lift up and shove it with your knee."

Iris snorted, somehow not surprised the door had the same quirks as when her mother was young enough to work here. She lifted the handle, turning the key until it rotated. Her knee to the rough spot between the doors did the trick.

Several of the women closest to her glanced at the noise of cold metal shifting, then went right back to their conversational cover.

Iris reached far enough to depress the switches on the wall, bringing long rows of overhead lights to life. The three women stepped inside the echoing warehouse and pulled the doors shut behind them.

Chapter 14

Just as Iris expected, the broad cinderblock and concrete space hadn't changed since she worked her last shift a couple of years ago. Long silvery pipes ran from the edges of the room to a central collection area, all of it driven by a vast boiler built halfway through the back wall. Raw maple sap took the long journey through those pipes, picking up heat and shedding water as steam, coming out the other side as the prized driver of Maple Ridge's tourist economy.

Pallets of several sizes of containers stood against the wall to the left, near a tall door that rolled up toward the ceiling. Supplies waiting for a late winter harvest Iris doubted would be coming this year. She'd spent plenty of February and March hours after school learning how the whole contraption worked.

The right wall held all the tools for working in the rows of huge old maple trees on the outskirts of town. Short, tubular metal spiles to tap through the bark, metal buckets with curved lids to collect the sap. Axes, handsaws, and chainsaws to work on the trees themselves.

After more early morning shifts than she cared to count, Iris could have started up the boiler to warm the women and kids inside the store in about two minutes. She wouldn't even have to go outside to add wood as long as the power held out. And Haga, Dale, Matt, or Bill and Rita Hicks would spot the steam venting in about two seconds.

To no one's surprise, all the food and useful supplies from the store - supplies a starving town desperately needed - were piled up in front of the empty bottles and jars.

No matter what the consequences, Iris wasn't about to let everyone stay hungry and thirsty on top of being cold.

"Grab as much water as you can carry," she said, picking up a case of cheese and crackers. "Won't be the most nutritious breakfast, but we'll do our best."

"This is where they make the maple syrup?" Gena said.

"Most of it," Iris's mother said. "They have a little hand driven demonstration area around back, all kinds of fire and steam, but that's just for education. And for the tourists. They can run gallons a day through here."

When the three of them stepped back into the store with their gifts of food and water, everyone else gave up pretending not to notice.

"Did you get the heat started?" one of the women called.

"We can't do that," Iris said. "At least not while it's light out. I'm sorry. That boiler vents to the outside, and we'd have to feed it out there after a couple of hours. They'd know we can get in the back. Drink and eat fast as you can, and we'll hide what's left."

"A full belly won't mean much if they take it out on our kids and our men."

Iris didn't recognize the woman who'd spoken, not with

a pink scarf covering most of her face. Her mother did.

"I don't know about you, Nancy," Carol Rutherford said, her voice sharp. "But I don't intend to sit quietly by and let them push all of us around. I doubt they're taking our men and boys out for some kind of charity run."

Nancy crossed her arms, refusing the water Gena held out.

"There *is* a back door in case you forgot. I doubt *they* forgot about the food and water stashed in there for a hot second."

"We saw the door, ma'am," Gena said. Iris knew that smile was full of venom. "Thank you for the reminder. Please do let us know if you have a better idea than what we're doing."

Iris watched several women and a few children step toward Gena, each of them making a point of thanking her. She couldn't tell if Nancy scowled before she walked away.

Iris did recognize one of her middle school teachers. Ms. Blevins nodded her thanks at the cheese and crackers. Her round, cheery face looked strange without a smile.

"Probably taking our men down to Wolf Branch. Rumor is they got plenty of food put by. My nephew Zach heard they went down there a couple of times already, scouting the place out."

Iris shivered, meeting Gena's worried gaze. The idea of an attack on Wolf Branch brought the flames surging in her mind again. This time tinted with black and red. Flames her father and the other men might be dragged into, along with a whole community that didn't deserve the violence.

"Whatever they're doing," Iris said, "we need to figure out some way to fight when we can. No matter what that Nancy says."

Ms. Blevins laughed, a low, throaty sound Iris remembered well.

"Nancy Nelson is pissed she's not out there with a rifle bossing everyone around like her rotten boy Matt, not that he seems to be treating her any better than the rest of us. Rita Hicks doesn't like Nancy any more than I do, or she would be. I'd watch that one."

Food and water shared out, the three women ducked back into the warehouse.

"Hate to say it," Iris's mother said, "but Nancy's got a point about the door. I saw your key, but I'd bet they've got it locked from the outside. Wonder if we could cut the power? Raising it by hand would take a lot longer. Probably be a lot louder, too."

"Looks like we could jam it." Gena stepped forward, toward the boxy metal housing for the door's motor. Chains looped out and up to the top of the massive door.

A cold deeper than the air around her twisted up through Iris, from her feet to her heart.

"Wait," she said. "Not now. Not yet."

"They can just walk right…" Gena's forehead wrinkled when her eyes met Iris's. "What did you see?"

"I didn't see anything, not really. But this isn't the right time. We need to get back out there, get everything hidden."

Her mother nodded. "You're probably right. They won't set out on their grand men-only mission without making sure we all know about it."

All three women pocketed a makeshift weapon when they passed by the maintenance bench on the way out. A long screwdriver, a chisel, a thin steel icepick.

Iris had no doubt all three of them would use them the second they got the chance.

Chapter 15

By the time the barn doors jerked, squealed, and rolled open several hours later, all evidence of their thin breakfast was hidden under the checkout counter along with the system monitor panel. Bill and Rita Hicks strolled in as the small bit of heat generated by so many bodies floated out.

"Glad to see you settling in," Bill said, his gaze moving slowly over the group. "Happy to say most of your men are doing the same. I understand you'd like the heat turned on in here."

Haga walked up behind him, staring at Iris with a half smile. Dale stayed a few paces behind her, face red and stony. Iris knew she wasn't the only one who noticed three guards outside, Matt's smug face among them, making sure their rifles were visible.

"Heat would help, sure," Mrs. Williams said. "So would letting us out of here."

"Well, we can't do that just yet." Bill spoke as if he were comforting a small child. "But I'll see what I can do about that boiler. Dale."

Dale glared at everyone close by as he followed Mr. Hicks through the same door Iris had carefully locked.

"Everyone doing all right in here?" Rita Hicks said. She walked through the store, eyes constantly moving. Haga stayed by the open door. "We'll get you all something to eat and drink here in a little bit. Coffee if you want it."

"We're going to need restrooms before long," Ms. Blevins said. "The kids especially."

Rita shrugged. "There's the public restroom around the side of the building, but I'm afraid those pipes are busted. Cold weather and no power most days, you know. Might be able to take you in shifts back to the warehouse toilets. Assuming those are working, of course."

Everyone jumped at a rumble from the overhead vents. Barely warmed air flowed after a few seconds, along with the singed smell of dust in the pipes.

"There now," Rita said. "That will get warmer before long. You just sit tight and I'll check on those toilets."

She glanced at Haga, then joined her husband in the warehouse. Haga walked into the middle of the store. She didn't have her rifle, but her hand rested on a handgun in a holster around her waist. She brought the orange flames with her, and at least to Iris, the stink of gunpowder, burning flesh, and death.

"How long are we going to be in here, Haga?" Iris said. "It's almost one o'clock and these kids haven't had anything to eat. We'll need more than food and toilets."

"Don't know why you think I'm going to tell you any such thing, Iris. You know as well as I do you're asking the wrong person. We all got more important things to worry about right now."

Ignoring her racing heart - and her rational mind screaming at her to stop - Iris stepped forward. A stronger force drove her on. She spoke quietly enough that no one else could hear.

"Like what's going to happen to you when the little raiding party is over, maybe? Do you really believe you won't get used up just like the rest of us?"

Haga's eyes narrowed for a second, then a slow smile broke across her face.

"If I didn't know better, I'd think you were trying to distract me for some reason. Trying to start something you might not be willing to finish. I know you're smarter than that. Least you think you are."

Iris shrugged, much like Rita had, frowning a little.

"I guess we'll see who's smart in the end. Or thinks she is."

Haga raised one eyebrow. She looked away from Iris, but directly at her mother and Gena.

"Everybody takes big chances in times like these. Might want to make sure you can live with the results."

The double doors to the warehouse swung open with a metallic squeak, breaking the silence all over the room.

"All right," Rita Hicks called, standing in the doorway with her arms crossed. "Both toilets back there are working. Can't say they're clean, but they work. Figure out who needs to go and get moving."

Haga locked gazes with Iris again, ignoring everyone else moving around them. She only turned when Rita Hicks stood beside the two of them.

"If you'd be so kind as to keep an eye on everyone, Haga, I'll make sure breakfast is on the way."

"Will do, Mrs. Hicks. Wouldn't want any unfortunate accidents over here."

Everyone started moving at once when the front doors finally rolled closed behind Mrs. Hicks and the two guards outside. Iris hung back with Gena and her mother, watching Haga station herself by the doors to the warehouse. Dale and Bill Hicks were still back there.

"Can you explain to me why you're trying to piss her off?" Gena said. "I didn't have to grow up here to see she's not exactly stable."

"I don't know what to tell you." Iris held out her arms. Gena resisted for several seconds before she stepped into a hug. "You know how we both felt like we had to come up here? Something like that."

"So far they haven't noticed we can get back there," Iris's mother said. "At least we have that one advantage. I'm more worried about that Dale than Haga."

"You should be," Iris said. "And his buddy Matt Nelson. Dale made me uncomfortable every time I saw him back in school, and every police and sheriff's department in the region is well acquainted with Matt. Giving those two rifles is about the dumbest move I ever heard of."

The restrooms were awful, but functional enough. Grubby toilets still flushed. Cracked, stained sinks still drained. After making a grand show of leaving fresh boxes of rough toilet paper and coarse brown paper towels, Mr. Hicks busied himself and Dale with inspecting the boiler instead of keeping too close an eye on the quiet parade of women and children relieving themselves.

Mr. Hicks sauntered out of the warehouse when everyone was finished, locking the door behind him. Haga smirked as she left, and Dale continued to scowl as he walked close on her heels. Nothing had gone as badly as Iris feared.

The "breakfast" Rita Hicks returned with was another story.

Chapter 16

Boys not old enough to be out of high school wheeled cafeteria carts into the store under Matt Nelson's scornful gaze nearly an hour later. The way the boys picked up the tall pots and wide pans without oven mitts or even gloves, along with the way they refused to meet anyone's eyes, confirmed her worst fears.

They dropped everything unceremoniously on the checkout counter, along with bags of paper plates, plastic bowls, spoons, cups, and cafeteria napkins. They hurried out without a word or backward glance. Matt grinned and bowed low, sweeping one arm toward the food before he walked out

"Best we could do on short notice," Rita said with a broad smile. "Things are moving fast now that they finally got started. We'll have better for everyone before many days have passed."

Rita walked out, leaving the guards to roll the doors shut behind her. Before they did, Haga leaned in long enough to catch Iris's gaze. She raised a huge mug of something that steamed in the cold air.

"What was that all about?" Iris's mother said when the doors finally closed.

"Somehow I doubt anything they brought us will steam like that."

The first women to carefully lift the lids confirmed her suspicions. What Rita had finally delivered at two in the afternoon consisted of a solid mass of congealed oatmeal, a yellowish mess of what resembled rubbery scrambled eggs, and black coffee. Every bit of it as cold as the air outside.

"What the hell did they do?" Ms. Blevins said, her cheeks flushed. "Leave it sitting out on the street all day?"

"Probably did just that." Nancy Nelson had removed her pink scarf but still clutched it in one hand. Now nothing hid the permanent frown etched into her flesh when she glared at Iris. "That's what comes of giving them trouble."

"I'll invite you to skip it then," Iris's mother said. She opened the other containers, revealing more of the same. "Can't do much about these eggs, but a little hot water from the boiler and a touch of maple syrup will do the rest a world of good."

Everyone moved at once, getting the children settled and eating first thing. The oatmeal and coffee were better than expected after a few modifications. Hardly anyone touched the whatever was supposed to pass for eggs.

Full bellies and the room shifting from frigid to comfortable to hot left heads nodding despite the coffee and fear. Gena and Iris leaned against the counter, away from everyone but Mrs. Williams still perched on her chair. Like the women and many of the kids, they'd taken off their winter coats.

Gena spoke Iris's thoughts before she could.

"We're a lot easier to manage if we're all sound asleep. They may as well have drugged the food."

"No point in that if they can just heat us half to death," Iris said. "I hate to say it, but it's probably better if everyone is calm until we figure something out."

"Wouldn't hurt you to take a nap." Gena kissed Iris's cheek. "I'm going to go stretch my legs, look around a little bit. Maybe check out our tool supply back there. I think I spotted a machete."

She held out her hand, waiting for Iris to drop the keys into it.

"Watch that back door. And don't hurt yourself, city girl."

Gena winked, then walked as quietly as she could through the rows of dozing and sleeping bodies.

Iris tilted her head from side to side, trying to loosen her painfully tight shoulders. She closed her eyes against the glare of the overhead lights.

Just for a second…

Mrs. Williams's voice and hand on her shoulder startled Iris out of an unexpected sleep.

"There's some kind of noise under here." She pointed to the security terminal Iris had checked earlier.

Iris rubbed her grainy eyes, trying to focus on her watch. She hadn't noticed what time Gena went back there, but her body felt stiff enough to have slept for an hour rather than a few seconds. Almost four o'clock.

She heard the low beeping then.

Iris pulled the screen out, blinking at the blue words against the gray background.

Connection Established. System Normal.

A clammy knot clenched her gut, making her regret the late meal.

"Did anything else change? Any other noises?"

"No, honey," Mrs. Williams said, now sounding

worried herself. "Did someone get that security system started back up?"

Iris shook her head, trying to think around a nagging headache. The room was hot enough now that sweat ran down her back and between her breasts.

"Maybe. This could be automated, but I can't risk it."

Everyone Iris could see either had their eyes closed or might as well have. Only her mother stared back at her, tense and alert. She got to her feet and met Iris at the double doors leading to the warehouse.

"What's wrong?"

"The security system is back on. Or it might be. Right now we have to get Gena."

Her mother's eyes widened. "I didn't see her go back there!"

"Stand behind me, block that camera in the corner." Iris knew no one watching any of the cameras would miss the two of them leaving the room, but none of that mattered. "She said she was going to look for a machete."

Iris pushed one of the doors slowly, keeping the noise to a whispering scrape. The room beyond was dark and quiet except for the low rumble of the boiler working overtime.

Gena didn't have a flashlight.

"Wait by the door," Iris said, grabbing her mother's hand. "If someone comes in the front, I'll need to know."

Her mother stepped forward, peering into the darkness.

"If Gena's back there, they've already got her. She'd have to see the door open. Why would she have the lights turned out?"

Painfully brittle fear froze all of Iris's muscles, and she bit her lip to keep from throwing up a mass of overly sweet maple syrup, coffee, and oatmeal.

Why? Why had she brought Gena up here?

"I have to try, Mom. There may still be time."

A scream rang out in the darkness, piercing through the terror in Iris's heart and mind.

Gena.

Chapter 17

Before Iris could move, her mother flipped all the warehouse lights on.

The dusty concrete floor was covered with too many footprints to show which way Gena had gone, but Iris caught movement against the right wall. Near all those axes and saws.

"You *bitch*!"

Dale staggered toward the middle of the warehouse, clutching his bloody right hand to his chest. His rifle bounced uselessly on his back.

"Gena!"

Iris sprinted forward, aiming toward the flash of blonde hair darting behind the row of supplies.

Dale turned toward Iris, face red and furious, trying to grab his rifle with his left hand. More blood poured from the fist still held against his body.

Everything around Iris slowed, too bright and loud, bringing every detail into hard reality around her.

Dale's mouth opening, chest rising.

Neck muscles straining as he fought to grab the rifle with his dumb hand.

Dust motes floating in the endless space between her and Gena.

Her mother's pounding footsteps.

Gena's fierce and raging eyes as she walked up behind Dale.

The sharp blade of the axe flashing over her shoulder.

The furious scream through her blood-ringed mouth as she swung.

The meaty thunk of steel sinking into flesh where Dale's neck met his shoulder.

Dale's gurgling cry, the only sound he made before his dead body hit the concrete.

Iris didn't realize she'd skidded to a stop until her mother crashed into her. She landed hard enough to jar the world back into normal time.

"Gena!" her mother shouted, sprawled out beside Iris.

Gena didn't look at either of them. She knelt beside Dale, shoving him until she could yank the rifle away. She picked up the axe when she stood and turned.

She didn't seem to notice the blood she streaked over her hands and shoulder when she slipped the rifle's strap across her own back.

"What happened?" Iris said, gasping for breath. On top of her fear, she'd knocked her wind out when she fell.

Gena wiped her hands absently on her jeans, then reached down to help Iris and her mother stand.

"Must have been back here waiting. After I walked across, he turned the lights out. Blinded me with a huge flashlight. Wait, I need to get it."

She turned away, and Iris glanced at her mother. Iris could feel where she'd scraped her own chin and cheek, but her mother's face was unmarked. And her eyes were as wide and shocked as Iris's had to be.

Gena kicked Dale over again, reaching toward something that clattered against the floor. She grabbed a heavy black flashlight almost as long as her forearm. Iris hadn't seen an old one like that since she was a little girl exploring in her grandfather's basement.

"Did he hurt you?" Iris said, trying not to look at the spreading pool under Dale's body.

"I don't think so." Gena stared at her palms, then wiped them on her jeans again. "I saw you open the door and I just…I lost my head."

Iris let all her breath out again, the closest thing she could manage to a laugh.

Dale was the one…the one who nearly lost…

Gena wiped at her mouth, frowning at the blood there.

"He grabbed me, had his hand over my mouth. Dragged me toward that back corner, pushed me down." She rubbed the back of her head. "Knocked my skull pretty good. Smacked him a few times, kept him from getting what he wanted. I was afraid others were with him, so I didn't scream until I saw you."

Iris reached out and touched Gena's trembling hand, then slipped hers around the axe handle. Gena let go and went back to rubbing her crimson-stained leg.

"I bit him," she said. "Right through his hand. Had to spit it out back there."

She grabbed her stomach and covered her mouth.

"Still taste… I can still taste it."

Iris caught Gena before she could fall, easing her to her knees just as the retching started. Iris's mother knelt beside them, holding Gena's hair back and away from the chunky brown vomit.

When Gena sat back, still spitting and breathing hard,

Iris's mother got up and walked over to the food stash. She brought back an armful of bottles of water and Coke.

"Here hon, this will help," she said, holding the water out.

Gena filled her mouth and spit into the mess a few times. When she reached for the Coke, her hand shook worse than before.

"They'll notice. That he's gone. What… What are we going to do?"

"Get you out of here," Iris said. She hugged Gena close. "We're armed now, thanks to you."

Chapter 18

WHEN THEY STARTED toward the bathroom to let Gena wash up, the flames raged hot and bright inside Iris's mind.

"We can't do this right now," she said, shaking her head. "We may be running out of time."

Iris's mother looked at the axe over Iris's shoulder, the rifle over Gena's.

"Wait here just one minute. We're gonna need more than this."

She set out at a fast pace back toward the tree trimming supplies, detouring wide around Dale's messy remains.

"You're bleeding," Gena said. She touched Iris's undamaged cheek, turning her face to the side.

"That might help us. If everyone out there sees what went on, they'll be willing to fight."

Gena and Iris walked forward to help with the load of weapons Carol Rutherford carried. Three more axes, several loops of loose chainsaw blade, and four of the stout machetes Gena had been after in the first place.

"That's about all I could manage. Might want to send a couple of the others out to grab more."

Iris didn't bother trying to be as quiet walking back through to the front of the store as she had been going out back. If someone *was* watching the cameras, they were taking their sweet damn time responding.

Gasps floated through the women, followed by children's moans and cries. Before the shouted questions could really get started, Iris's mother stepped forward, drawing attention away from the bloodied younger women.

"Now listen. One of those guards was waiting back there in the dark. If we hadn't gone out when we did, he would have done his best to act out Rita's almighty biology whether Gena wanted him to or not." Fists on her hips, she turned her head to look at everyone. "And if Gena hadn't gone out there, how long do you think he would have waited before he came in here after us? After our little ones?"

"What did you *do*?" Nancy shouted, clutching her pink scarf to her throat.

"I killed him," Gena said. Her voice was calm and steady now, just like the hand that gripped Iris's. "Right before he would have used this to kill Carol and Iris so he could get back to trying to rape me."

She lifted the rifle, bloody strap and all, above her head before dropping it back into place.

Iris spoke into the silence.

"I think the security system is back on, but no one seems to be watching it. If they were, they'd be here by now. So they probably don't know Dale was even back there. We might have a little time to get ready, but not much."

Iris's old teacher, Ms. Blevins, stepped forward. The

tight set of her mouth was grim, but her eyes were bright. She nodded at the weapons.

"Are some of those things for us?"

"These and plenty more in the back," Iris said. She couldn't stop her own grim smile as Ms. Blevins pulled on thick winter gloves and took one of the loops of chainsaw blade, looking deceptively like a thick bicycle chain rather than a vicious cutting tool. "I think we need to get the kids close against the wall in the warehouse, right inside this door. Then we'll set up by the doors."

"And then what?" Nancy's voice rose to nearly a shriek. "Sit here and wait until they shoot us all to death? One assault rifle against a dozen, with all of us caught in the crossfire?"

Nancy glared at Iris's mother, not seeming to notice the whispers and sobs of children all around them. Iris forced herself not to say anything. She couldn't explain it to anyone besides Gena or her mother, but she knew, she *knew* there were nowhere near that many guards left outside.

Her sense of calamity, of whirling orange and gray catastrophe, had shifted away from Maple Ridge and down the mountain toward Wolf Branch.

Whatever disaster she'd been dreaming about was well underway.

"You do whatever the hell you want to, Nancy," Iris's mother said. "Maybe your boy will finally remember to sneak in at the last minute and rescue you, right? Until then, you keep out of the way and let us do whatever we can. If you don't, I'll tie you up and lock you in the bathroom myself."

All the other women moved then, either herding their kids toward the warehouse or walking through themselves to help gather what weapons they could.

Mrs. Williams left her perch beside the checkout counter. She stepped up beside Iris, face pale with high spots of color in her cheeks.

"Can I have one of those?" she said quietly, pointing to a machete.

Iris didn't have to ask if she was remembering the iron bar swung at her son's leg, or his scream as he collapsed.

She gave the blade to Mrs. Williams without a word.

Chapter 19

By the time Ms. Blevins thought to distribute boxes of maple candy to keep the children quiet and distracted, they were as ready as they could get.

The tree maintenance wall was nearly empty, with even the palm-sized spiles that normally drained sap out of the maple trees rounded up and shared around. Not nearly as sharp as the cutting tools, but Iris had nicked her winter-chilled fingers on the spouts and hooks more than enough to know they'd do some kind of damage.

Someone, Iris wasn't sure who, had taken the time to find an old gray tarp and used it to keep the kids from seeing what had really happened in the warehouse earlier. Someone else had jammed a long screwdriver through the chains that raised the warehouse door, keeping it from moving more than a few inches no matter who triggered the switch.

Several women arranged themselves out of sight on either side of the rolling front doors of the store. The others surrounded the group of kids gathered on the warehouse side of the passage between the two spaces.

Only Nancy Nelson had refused any kind of weapon. She hadn't resisted when Carol Rutherford told her to sit outside the bathroom door, then, and stay the hell out of the way. Iris wasn't the only one to keep an eye on the disagreeable woman on top of everything else she was trying to pay attention to.

Not nearly the preparations Iris or anyone else would have liked. But nowhere near as helpless as they'd felt - and been - only an hour before.

"How many do you think are out there?" Gena said in a low voice. She sat close beside Iris behind the checkout counter, where they could both watch the unchanging screen for the security system.

"One less, and a nasty one at that." Iris kissed Gena's cheek, finally scrubbed clean of the remains of Dale. "I get the feeling a lot of them are gone already."

"Down to Wolf Branch," Gena said, nodding. "That's what I feel like, too."

"So probably Haga, Rita Hicks. Maybe a few of the younger men."

"Do you really think they're arrogant enough to leave us here with so few watching us?"

Iris shrugged, wishing she had some way to honestly answer. To *know*.

"They've left us in here for a long time already. I'm sure if they suspected we could get into the warehouse, they would have left a guard back there. They're assuming we're weaker and more afraid than we are."

"And we may be assuming they're better prepared and organized than they are. But we have to be ready."

Those words, *they've left us in here for a long time*, echoed and rebounded in Iris's mind, getting louder and more angry with each repetition. How long had she left Gena out there while taking a nap?

How long had Gena had to fight off Dale and his filthy hands and mouth and everything else?

"I'm sorry, Gena. I shouldn't have left you out there alone for so long."

Gena turned her head and shoulders toward Iris, shaking her head.

"What? You mean when I… When he was back there?"

Iris closed her eyes, wishing she could banish the horrible images from her mind.

"Not only did I drag you up here into mountaintop hell, but I sat up here, right here, sound asleep while you were back there by yourself with that worthless pile of shit."

Gena blinked, but she smiled instead of drawing away.

"I was only out there for a few minutes, Iris. Pretty much long enough to walk across the floor and look at the tools. Wish I'd grabbed one before he turned the lights out, but he ended up the same either way."

"A few minutes?" Iris rubbed her stiff neck with one hand. "Really? I feel like I was asleep sitting up for ages."

"There might be a lot more to that than a quick nap we could all use." Gena pulled Iris forward, digging her strong fingers into the knots around Iris's neck and shoulders. "You didn't abandon me, no more than I would have abandoned you to drive up here all by yourself. I'm exactly where I want to be. Today and every day."

Iris closed her eyes for a second, wanting more than anything to let Gena soothe her to sleep. But the weariness that surged through her mind and body were much too heavy and deep to give in to.

"Listen, are you… Did it bother you, what you had to do?"

Gena half-smiled, but her eyes didn't look happy this time.

"You mean did I mind nearly chopping that asshole's head off? I won't say I'm perfectly fine, no. When we finally get out of here, I expect I'll have enough sleepless nights to make up for your dreams and then some."

Iris leaned back and put her arm around Gena's shoulders, wishing she could make the whole thing go away and never bother Gena or anyone else trapped in this nightmare again.

"But for now?"

"For now, I'm not thinking about it. I might have to do a lot worse before this is over. I can't fall apart until then, and neither can you."

Iris nodded, then glanced back at the monitor.

Her breathing, heart, and all her thoughts jerked to a halt.

The gray screen and blue words had vanished. Instead she saw several tiny windows, like miniature television screens. Most of the scenes seemed as frozen as her body, showing the boiler out back, the chained doors in front of the store, the empty parking lot between the sugar barn and the middle school. Other locations around and inside other buildings in town, places Iris had never noticed cameras before.

Or where Bill and Rita had recently added them.

But she also saw women shifting around inside the warehouse.

And she saw herself and Gena, the tops of their heads obviously in range of a camera designed to watch whoever ran the cash register.

"The screen," she croaked, her throat tight and dry. "The whole thing is on now."

Gena caught her breath and tensed against Iris.

"That's the whole town, isn't it? Where is that coming from?"

Iris shook her head, trying to get her numb feet and legs to move.

"I never saw that before, only the inside of the store and the warehouse. It could be some kind of default view. I promise you someone else can see it all, too."

Just as Iris dragged herself up with Gena's help, one of the tiny scenes finally changed. People walking in front of the middle school. Haga and Rita Hicks clear even at barely an inch high.

Their guns every bit as visible before the screen went black.

"Get ready!" Iris shouted. "They're coming!"

"Remember they don't know we're armed," Gena said, her voice lower but no less urgent. "All they can see is we moved around. We can still surprise them if we're careful."

Besides shouts to warn the women by the warehouse doors, everyone was surprisingly quiet. Iris held the assault rifle, leaving Gena to carry the same axe. Sally Lee, a neighbor not far from Iris's parents, crouched behind Gena with a handsaw.

They stood just inside the rolling doors, with other women across from them, armed and ready. Mrs. Williams watched Iris, machete gripped low against her legs.

"I'll turn the lights out as soon as they move the chain," Iris said, low enough for only the women around the door to hear. "The sun went down a while ago, so they'll be as blind as we are. Hopefully more."

At a metallic rattle outside, Iris took a deep breath and squeezed Gena's hand.

She reached forward and flipped the row of switches. Out in the warehouse, her mother did the same before she closed the double doors.

They waited in darkness.

Chapter 20

One of the doors creaked and rolled a few inches to the right.

Frigid dry air invaded the silent room, and brilliant white light cut through the black in front of Iris's eyes.

The beam aimed straight back to the far wall, over the closed doors to the warehouse. Down along the floor, left and right across the empty store shelves pushed back out of the way.

"Not sure what you think you can do here," Haga said, still outside the door. "Take all of us out and walk yourself down that mountain, I suppose."

Silence, even from the warehouse and the group of children.

"The warehouse door is still closed," Rita Hicks said, anger and frustration clear in her voice. "Unless Dale's dumb ass managed to kill them all, they're in there."

Iris forced her finger to stay loose, flat against the loop of the trigger guard, no matter how badly she wanted to open fire. Despite her strong feeling almost all the men were gone, she had no idea what waited outside.

Haga spoke quietly, but with the same irritated edge.

"Go on, then. You were full of piss and bluster about how you'd keep all us *females* safe when Bill rolled out. Now's your chance."

The light bobbled for a second, then the door squealed and moved sideways again. The blunt end of a short, modern flashlight slipped into sight. Propped on top of the hand holding the light was a hand holding a gun.

Iris forced herself to breathe, tried to will everyone around her to do the same.

After a few shuffling steps forward, skinny arms clad in faded blue corduroy came into view. Iris was certain they belonged to Bob Kaiser, one of the men she'd seen gathered around Bill Hicks that morning. Bob's local claim to fame might normally be hauling tourists around the vast ring of maple trees in a creaky wagon full of hay, for an absurdly expensive fee.

But right now, he was armed, wanting to impress Bill and everyone else, and walking right into the middle of their little group of women and children.

"Don't be stupid, now," Bob called out, his voice booming in the nearly empty store. "Hiding out like a bunch of cowards won't help."

He moved one hand away from the gun and waved the light around, never quite reaching the sides where Iris and the other women stood. More of those shuffling steps took him away from Iris.

Toward the light switches.

Bob swung the hand with the flashlight to his right, but before the beam touched the small group, Iris heard a faint metallic shift.

Right before Bob's scream drowned out everything else.

The light jerked along with his body to the right.

Iris barely had time to register blood surging under the

chainsaw blade around Bob's wrist before he brought the gun around.

Mrs. Williams stepped forward and swung the machete.

A bright flash and bang.

Bob fell to his knees, dropping both the flashlight and the gun.

Another light from outside flared toward the back of this store just in time to show Bob's kicking legs as he was dragged out of sight.

"That's enough!" Haga shouted, with Rita's bellow close behind.

"Every last *one* of you will pay for this!"

The light focused on the handgun, about five feet away from Iris on the floor. None of them could reach it without stepping into range of Haga's assault rifle, and probably more than that.

But no one outside could walk in without ending up like Bob. Moaning mixed with screaming himself hoarse even when something - or someone - was obviously pressing on his throat.

Iris wasn't sure whether she hoped more for the machete or the chainsaw blade.

Whoever held the light outside stepped closer, the bright circle covering most of the room now. And no doubt that the next person to walk in would shoot to either side of the doors before setting one foot inside.

Shouts rang out from the warehouse, loud enough that even Bob shut up. Gena pressed up tight against Iris's back, trembling, and she didn't have to say a word.

Iris's mother was back there. And the children.

The flashlight beam lit the double doors as they shuddered, then metal squealed when one opened barely an inch.

"Gun! They have a *gun*!"

The door slammed hard enough to rattle in its frame, and Nancy Nelson's shrieking voice stopped.

Bob's moaning started up again.

"Dale's dumb ass got inside after all." Rita still sounded like she was well away from the barn doors. She also sounded strangely calm. "Managed to lose his gun, maybe his worthless life. Not much of a surprise there. Guess we'll have to deal with him when this is all over. Unless you already took care of him for us. Then we'll just have to say thank you."

Iris barely had time to wonder why Rita was suddenly so damn chatty before she heard a grunt and a metallic clatter from behind her. Gena's body twisted, then disappeared.

She turned in time to see Gena step over Sally's dropped handsaw and dart out the open side door, axe still in her hands.

Chapter 21

I_RIS WALKED AWAY_ from the middle of the store - from the handgun on the floor and Bob's moans and the other three women - without a backward glance. Gena's insistence that she'd only been in the warehouse alone for a few minutes hadn't entirely left her mind.

She wasn't about to leave Gena on her own again. Iris raised the assault rifle and stepped through the door.

Cold starlight outside helped her see a little better, but not much.

Rita Hicks off to the side, well away from the barn doors.

Two young boys and a girl, surely still in high school down in Wolf Branch during less insane times. One of the boys held a huge flashlight toward the inside of the store.

All of them turning toward where Iris stood.

In between, Haga with one arm around Sally Lee's neck, dragging her backward, the other hand over her mouth.

Gena with the axe raised over her shoulder, moving to get behind Haga.

Iris saw Rita realize Haga had brought more than a hostage along with her, and at a gesture from her, the boy swung the light around.

Iris yelled as loud as she could, breath she felt like she'd been holding for weeks exploding out.

"Get down!"

All she saw before she opened fire, all that mattered, was Gena lunging forward toward the frozen ground.

Iris didn't stop until the stinking hot gun was empty and the bolt locked open.

The boy's light bounced and rolled, ending up pointing toward the partly open door of the store. Iris crouched beside the building, trying to hide and see into the darkness.

"Gena!"

"I'm here." Gena's harsh whisper cut through more moans than Bob Kaiser could have managed in his prime. "We have to get their guns."

A light from inside the store traced a jagged path along the floor and outside. A few seconds later, all the overhead lights went on, along with several big floodlights above Iris's head.

Before she managed to turn away, Iris saw what was left of two of the young guards who'd been standing beside Rita. One of the boys huddled on the ground, hands over the back of his head. He'd thrown his gun far out of reach.

Rita herself was still breathing, but she wouldn't be much longer. From the looks of her chest and stomach, she didn't have enough left to be bleeding for much longer, either.

For one horrible second, Iris thought the blood covering Gena's arms and hands was her own. That she'd miscalculated how fast Gena moved and had managed to hit the last person on earth she wanted to hurt.

But her eyes finally focused enough to realize Gena was trying to cover the wound in Sally's shoulder. Sally herself sprawled across Haga's chest and stomach.

"Get the gun, Iris." Gena moved Sally forward as gently as she could, stopping at each sharp intake of air. "Under her."

Iris shook her head, trying to force her brain to re-engage so it could slow her furious heartbeat. Could this possibly be over? She didn't see anyone else or hear movement she couldn't explain.

But part of her remained convinced that danger waited just outside the bright circle of light.

Iris pulled herself up, bracing against the building. The women who'd been waiting inside the store stood around Rita Hicks.

No one's face or eyes showed the slightest trace of pity or compassion.

Haga watched Iris, her own eyes bright. Her face deathly pale and splattered with blood. The pattern of bullet holes across her chest and the dark stain spreading underneath her said all Iris needed to know. And more than she ever wanted to remember.

She leaned over to help get Sally to her feet, hot tears surging up at Sally's whimpering cries.

"I'm sorry," Iris whispered. "I didn't mean to hit you, Sally."

Sally tried to smile. "You really think I'd prefer Rita's tender mercies? Or the one who dragged me out here?"

"She tried to get down," Gena said, walking Sally over and helping her sit against the wall. "Haga tried to use her as a shield. She's not going anywhere, but get her gun. We don't know who's still out there or when the others will come back."

Iris forced herself to focus on the low conversation of the other women, Bob's moans and complaints, the noise of her own footsteps on the gravel. Anything to avoid hearing the gurgling noise from Haga's chest when she tried to breathe.

"You want me to turn you over?" Iris said, finally looking into Haga's reddened eyes. "Or you want to do that yourself?"

Haga's voice came out weak and breathless.

"Whatever the hell you think you need to do, Iris. You'll be glad to know I can't feel a damn thing past my shoulders anyway."

"I'm not glad about any of this." Iris squatted, trying not to inhale the meaty, metallic scent mixed with the sharp fumes of Haga's bladder letting go. "Except getting away from here and from you."

She gripped Haga's shoulder, raising her up enough to pull the rifle loose. Iris nearly dropped it when she realized the length of cold metal was coated in everything that was leaking out of the dying woman. She gritted her teeth, ignoring Haga's grunts, and yanked the gun and strap free.

Haga stared up at Iris, her words even harder to hear when she spoke again.

"Kill me then. Bullet in my head, knife at my throat. Whatever you got."

Iris stood, picking up Gena's axe along with the rifle. After a long look around - Sally's face twisted in pain, the other women walking slowly out from the warehouse, her mother's furious eyes - she leaned both weapons against the wall beside Sally and Gena. She returned to Haga's side and met her gaze.

A single handgun shot rang out, and Iris knew Rita Hicks had breathed her last. Someone in that circle of women had more compassion than she did at that moment. Iris didn't move or break eye contact with Haga.

"I don't have anything for you, Haga. You can bleed to death or freeze to death. Either one is kinder than what you were going to help them do to the rest of us."

Chapter 22

THE BOY CROUCHED on the ground turned out to be Jessie Estep, an unwilling participant, or at least that's what he claimed to be. The other women and a few kids verified that he'd been visiting from Laurel Pass a couple of hours away and got caught up in the whole mess.

The only thing Jessie wanted to know was how soon he could get to a phone and call his parents. No one knew when the phones had been cut, or whether it was done in Maple Ridge or somewhere else. The only thing they knew for certain was none of the digital lines or even the old copper lines worked. And mobile phones only gave fast busy signals.

What Iris and the other adults knew in their hearts was Jessie's parents would have long-since come to get him if they'd been able. But no one was willing to say that while looking into his worried blue eyes.

Jessie did help them get Rita's keys so all the women and children could take shelter in the middle school for the long, long night. Cots, mats from the gym, and sleeping bags let the kids get some real sleep, and most of the adults pretend to. After settling the children down in the echoing, warm gymnasium, they locked Bob Kaiser into one of the music rooms to muffle his noisy complaints.

No one argued with Iris about leaving Haga right where she was.

Or with Iris's mother about locking Nancy Nelson in a classroom not too far from Bob.

Jessie thought all the other men and older boys had gone on the raid down to Wolf Branch, but he was hardly part of Bill and Rita Hicks' inner circle. He had seen Mrs. Williams's boy Ben loaded into one of the pickup trucks, horribly swollen and useless knee or not.

The cold, bluish light visible through the windows around the top of the gym had warmed to pink and the pale yellow of a winter morning, but hadn't yet woken the others. Assuming any of them had actually gone to sleep. Iris guessed they were all enjoying the relative safety and comfort after walking away from a nightmare.

She and Gena had refused one of the gym mats. But after the last few days, being warm in a big sleeping bag, together, and safe as they could get felt like paradise.

"They probably took Ben to make sure he didn't try to help us," Iris said, snuggled as close to Gena as she could manage.

"That or using him as bait. I don't mean to sound that way, but I didn't see a whole lot of kindness out of anyone who was with Bill and Rita Hicks. How are we going to get out of here?"

Iris shook her head. Even though the huge room had been dark all night, she hadn't wanted to close her eyes. The images that flashed up as soon as she tried had her terrified she'd never sleep again.

"When the others are awake, or admitting they are, we'll go see if our van is still there. They might not have thought to take it with them on their grand raid. We can get Sally down the mountain at least. There's a hospital in Wolf Branch. Not exactly a major medical center, but better than what we can dig up out of the school nurse's office."

"Assuming Wolf Branch isn't a disaster by now," Gena said, her voice low and harsh. "Your father said those assholes had enough explosives to destroy the back road, didn't he? Or we could meet Bill and his glorious raiding party coming back up."

Gena didn't seem to realize how tightly she was gripping Iris's hand. Iris stroked her hair, kissing her forehead and both cheeks.

"We'll face whatever comes. They don't expect us to be out of the sugar barn, much less armed."

The sense of something horrible happening in Wolf Branch, whirling gray and orange heartbreak, hadn't entirely left Iris. But part of her - the same part that drove her to bring the paintings out of her mind and into reality - was certain Wolf Branch and the people who lived there survived. And that they would thrive.

Both jumped at a voice out of the gloomy darkness.

"I hate to disturb you," Ms. Blevins said. "I thought I heard you talking."

Iris sat up, not liking the worried tone in her former teacher's voice.

"We're awake. What's wrong? Something on the road?"

One of the women who lived closest to the main road into town had volunteered her house for the closest they could get to a guard outpost overnight. She and two others had spent the night with walkie-talkies liberated from Rita Hicks and Haga.

After several seconds of quiet shifting and brief flashes with a soft handheld light, Ms. Blevins sat beside Iris.

"Not the road. No word from there. It's Sally Lee. Her shoulder, it's still soaking through every kind of bandage we put on it, no matter how tight. She's cold but she's pouring sweat, doesn't seem to know where she is. And her poor little heart is just pounding."

Iris rubbed her eyes, wishing she'd at least tried to sleep. Their few hours of quiet and calm were over before anyone was ready.

"Okay, we can't wait. We'll walk down to the house, see if the van is still there. If it is, we'll get her and as many of the kids as we can out of here. Can you try to keep everyone quiet until we get back, Ms. Blevins?"

Ms. Blevins snorted. "I'll do what I can, at least until Bob Kaiser wakes up and starts his moaning again. But only if you drop the Ms. Blevins nonsense. My name is Lucy."

Iris was surprised by the smile on her own face.

"I'll do my best, Lucy."

Chapter 23

THE QUIET, nerve-straining walk through Maple Ridge chilled Iris more than the frigid wind driving stray bits of snow. The same streets, shops, houses, even the trees she knew so well had taken on threatening new life in the last twenty-four hours. Every leaf skittering down the sidewalk, creaking branch against heavy clouds overhead, and especially a few open doors rattling and slamming in the wind sent her heart pounding.

The deserted town left Gena and Iris's mother every bit as jumpy. Iris carrying an assault rifle while her mother carried a handgun and Gena carried the axe only made things worse. A quick dash inside to get the van keys and too-fast drive back to the middle school was all any of them could manage.

Iris didn't think she had enough space in her mind and heart for more fear. Not until she saw a group huddled together against the wind and more snow in the parking lot between the school and the sugar barn. All women except Jessie Estep, the boy who'd managed to escape Rita Hicks with his life when hers ended. He stood close Ms.

Blevins - Lucy - and both turned and watched Iris drive up.

Her mother was out the door before Iris could get the van parked.

"What's going on?"

Mrs. Williams walked away from the group, one of the walkie-talkies clutched in her hand.

"They're hearing some kind of vehicle outside of town, probably more than one. No one can see them yet, so they're not sure who. But someone's on the way."

A bone-deep shudder unrelated to the cold tore through Iris. Gena's wind-reddened face paled, and she grabbed Iris's arm.

"Can *you* see anything, Iris? Like you you saw flames behind Haga when all this started?"

Instead of the swarm of black, gray, and flaming red tornadoes focusing behind Haga or Bill and Rita Hicks, Iris saw and felt them all around her. Whirling noise and fury threatened to consume all of Maple Ridge, then spread devastation out across the mountains, Virginia, and all the rest of the country.

"I see..." Iris gritted her teeth, trying to stop the chattering. "The nightmare. All around us."

"From the road?" Gena pulled Iris close and whispered into her ear. "Is it Bill and the rest?"

Iris forced cold air into her lungs and squeezed her eyes closed.

The horrible cyclones didn't fade or weaken, but light broke through the angry sky over their heads. Light that felt warmer than the December day, warmer than anything besides Gena had for many long months.

Light breaking through from the southeast. From Wolf Branch.

Yes.

From the road.

"I think…help. Trying to reach us. But danger all around."

Iris felt someone lean in close.

"They just said Nancy Nelson got loose while it was dark," her mother said. "Bob Kaiser, too. Not sure if they had help from outside or not. Is that what you're seeing, hon?"

The light concentrated, drawing to a blinding point so bright that Iris drew away and reached up to cover her eyes.

And opened her eyes facing the road out of Maple Ridge.

The rumble of engines reached her ears at the same time.

"Something's wrong, but I can't tell where. We can't stay out here."

Movement flashed at the last rise, some kind of vehicle, hard to make out in the thickening snow. Too far to tell if it was one of the trucks that had carried so many of their men and boys away.

Mrs. Williams jerked the radio to her ear.

"That's not them! It's not the trucks from Maple Ridge!"

Iris gripped her mother's hand.

"We're not safe out here, Mom. No matter who it is."

Gena started toward the group, Iris's mother close behind her. Iris herself stayed frozen, helpless, locked into dread of what her next few breaths would bring.

The vehicles rumbled closer, moving at a fast clip down the empty road. With the whole of Maple Ridge only a few blocks long, they'd be there in less than a minute.

Along with whatever held the terrible storms in Iris's mind.

"Let's get everyone inside," Iris's mother said, holding up both hands. "Just to be safe."

"Go," Iris whispered, unable to force her voice any louder.

The women took a few steps toward the middle school, then Mrs. Williams shouted.

"They brought an ambulance! We need to get Sally out here!"

Everyone turned, and Iris managed to move her head along with them. A bright white van, with the clear bulge of red lights on top, drove right behind a brown Wolf Branch police car. An old van not much different than hers followed, then several trucks.

A shot rang out, the bullet ricocheting off the bricks of the school building.

Three women whipped their rifles around, taking aim at the road.

"No!" Lucy Blevins cried. "They're from Wolf Branch!"

The next shot caught her in the chest.

Iris moaned as the police car, the ambulance, then the rest of the vehicles slammed on their brakes hard enough to squeal on the cold pavement.

She ducked behind her van, jerking the passenger door open. She grabbed her own rifle, making sure she stayed out of sight of the police car. And out of sight of the line of shops across the street.

Gena and her mother shouted, telling everyone to take cover. The next shot broke a window in the school, sending them running toward the sugar barn.

Iris expected the twisters to point the way, or the increasing light in her mind to let her know where the shooters were. They'd come from at least one of those shops, she was sure of that.

She saw the muzzle flash of the next one instead.

Iris raised the rifle, sighted the open door of the bakery, and fired once.

Bob Kaiser fell through the door, screaming.

Now the whirling maelstroms did shift, moving toward a clothing store on the opposite side of the street. Before Iris could adjust her aim, she heard a rifle burst from beside the school.

Glass shattered all along the storefront.

Two police officers jumped out of their car, crouching behind the open doors. An amplified voice roared through the snow.

"Do not fire! Lower your weapons! We're here to help you!"

Only the fierce wind broke the silence for several seconds. Then a wavering cry rose from the clothing store.

The voice from the police car boomed again.

"Please, lower your weapons. We know what you've been going through up here. We came to help."

Iris let the rifle slip from her shaking hands, back into the van's floorboard. She raised both arms and stepped forward, making sure Gena and her mother could see her.

The gray sky seemed close enough to touch, and the snow was settling in and getting serious. But all traces of the twisting storms had vanished. Iris only saw and felt the warm light all around her.

"It's over," she said, not bothering to wipe the tears from her cold cheeks. "It's finally over."

Chapter 24

AN ETERNITY PASSED while the officers from Wolf Branch searched and cleared the rest of the stores across from the middle school and the sugar barn. Iris stood hand in hand with her mother and Gena, struggling to hold on to what little reserves she had left.

Mrs. Williams waited close by, gripping an openly sobbing Jessie Estep in her arms. When Lucy Blevins's lifeblood splattered his chest and face, Jessie had grabbed one of the rifles and fired back. He'd stood by pale and silent while the police dragged Matt Nelson's lifeless body from the store.

When they'd carried Nancy Nelson out, wounded and wailing for Matt, Jessie didn't know how to stay strong anymore.

Bob Kaiser only managed to cry for help a few times before it was too late. Iris's former teacher and new friend Lucy hadn't had the chance to say a word.

The first person from Wolf Branch to cross the street was a compact, serious deputy named Melissa Wiggins.

Her dark features somehow managed to be sympathetic and angry at the same time.

"Did any of you hear shots from somewhere else? Or just from these stores?"

"Only those two locations that I heard," Iris said. "We haven't seen or heard anything since that stopped."

Deputy Wiggins nodded. "We're not seeing signs of anyone else. I think we should search the houses to be sure, but it would be best to get all of you down off the mountain before this snow really starts to pile up."

"One person inside needs to go now in that ambulance," Gena said. "She has a gunshot wound to her shoulder that won't stop bleeding."

"Now that we've got the area cleared, we'll get Dr. Hughes in there to have a look. A whole bunch of other folks came along to help as much as they could." She glanced at Nancy Nelson, now crouched on the steps up to the elementary school. No one besides the other officer was anywhere near her. "Unless someone else is hurt, there's plenty of room for two in the ambulance."

Iris's mother stepped forward, her smile chilly and terrifying.

"We'll just see how Nancy's doing and let you know."

Either missing or ignoring what Iris understood from her mother's tone, Deputy Wiggins turned toward the waiting vehicles and waved her arm. Under almost any other circumstances, Iris would have laughed at the way all the doors opened at once.

A woman wearing purple hospital scrubs under a heavy winter coat jumped out of the ambulance and ran toward them, thick dark blonde ponytail bouncing on her shoulders. She detoured toward Nancy, but Iris's mother moved faster. Iris and Gena followed as fast as they could, getting there at the same time as a young man dressed in the same scrubs.

"I'm Sandy Hughes," the woman said, grasping each of their hands. "This is my nurse Jeff."

"I'm glad to meet you, Sandy," Iris's mother said. "I suspect Nancy here was a big part of the violence we just had on top of every damn thing else. We have a good woman inside who's in much worse shape."

Sandy didn't even glance down.

"Understood. Take me to her."

"Let me ask you something before we go anywhere. Did you treat a man named Sid Rutherford down there in Wolf Branch? He was with that bunch from up here, but he wasn't one of them."

"I don't remember that name," Sandy said. "A whole bunch of men insisted on making the trip, though. He might be one of them."

Gena raised her head, looking at something behind Iris. She closed her eyes and smiled. When she opened them, she winked at Iris.

"I'll take you inside, Sandy."

Iris turned at the same time her mother did.

"Sid!"

Both women caught Sid Rutherford in a tight hug, nearly knocking him off his feet.

"It's okay now," he whispered. "It's all okay."

Similar quiet, joyful reunions filled the street, with women and children pouring out of the middle school into the street. After a few minutes, Iris stepped back, leaving her parents to a more intimate reconnection.

Her breath stopped when a man she'd never met before fell to his knees beside Lucy Blevins.

Iris turned away, nearly stepping right into another man, one she'd never even seen. He was nearly as tall as her father but not as lanky, with a thick red beard and curly red hair that caught the blowing snow.

In Iris's mind, the vivid shade danced in tiny shapes behind him, joined by matching bits of black, brown, and yellow.

"I'm sorry, I just about knocked you down," he said. He spoke with a flat Midwestern accent, and his smile was warm and friendly. "I probably need to stay the hell out of the way until someone tells me where to go."

Iris laughed, grinning back at him. Something inside her shifted, thawed, even as a fresh gust of wind seemed to drive the temperature down another ten degrees.

"What are you up here to do?" she said. "I'm Iris Rutherford."

He grasped her cold hand in both of his warm ones.

"Alex Collins. I need to get a look at the wind turbines, see if I can figure out why Wolf Branch isn't getting power from them anymore. But that can wait. The men we brought back up here said there are food stores? We should be able to get that loaded up today." He scowled and shook his head. "I mean, we'll leave enough for anyone who stays, of course. But we're glad to take in everyone for as long as you want."

"I think pretty much all of us will be ready to go as long as you have room for a pack of hunting dogs. There's food in the school, but the sugar barn is a little less crowded right now."

Too late, Iris remembered the remains of Haga and Rita Hicks. Both were in the same place, frozen solid from the looks of them. Alex didn't say a word as they approached the sugar barn's doors, but Iris knew she had to.

"We had a hard time up here last night. It went on a lot longer for some, but last night was the worst."

She'd thought he was in his mid-twenties, a few years older than Gena, but in that moment, tension and sadness around his blue eyes left Alex looking older than her parents.

"Last night was a rough one all around," he said in a soft voice. "Maybe we can tell each other about it someday."

They both turned at crunching footsteps on the gravel to see Gena walking toward them.

"Alex Collins," Iris said, "meet my girlfriend, Gena Wallace. My fiancé. Alex is going to help us get loaded up and get out of here."

A silvery flash caught Iris's eye when Alex reached for Gena's hand. A wedding ring with geometric shapes and ridges, sharp and bright and new.

"I'm glad to meet you, Gena. You'll meet my husband Etan tonight." He looked away and grinned, and his cold-flushed cheeks blushed a little deeper. "We've only been married a couple of weeks, still sounds strange to my ears."

Iris caught Gena's gaze, and she knew they were thinking of the same thing. The wedding party in Wolf Branch, back when they'd driven to Maple Ridge.

The deep, strong feeling they'd both had of their future being there, in that beautiful town by the Grasspe River.

The weave and pattern of colors in Iris's painting *Family*.

"Congratulations, Alex," Gena said, slipping her arm around Iris's waist. "I can't wait to meet him."

Another piece of their lives slipped gracefully into place.

ABOUT KARI

Kari Kilgore's wanderlust and imagination lead her all over the world on grand adventures. Her heart and family bring her home to her native Appalachian Mountains of Virginia. From that solid base, she and her husband Jason A. Adams bring those adventures to life in fiction.

Kari writes science fiction, fantasy, horror, and contemporary fiction, and she's happiest when she surprises herself. She lives at the end of a long dirt road in the middle of the woods with Jason, various house critters, and wildlife they're better off not knowing more about.

The Confidential Adventure Club

For Kari's exclusive free After The End stories, deleted scenes (including from the Storms of Future Past Series), discounts, early pre-sale releases, adorable pet photos, and a whole lot more not available anywhere else, visit The Confidential Adventure Club at www.smarturl.it/sofp-welcome.

Hope to see you there!

www.karikilgore.com
www.spiralpublishing.net

ALSO BY KARI KILGORE

I hope you enjoyed reading *Into the Storm* as much as I enjoyed writing it. For more of the Storms of Future Past series, including Book Four, *Fighting the Storm*, swing by www.smarturl.it/storms-series. Check out more of my fiction at www.karikilgore.com.

The Confidential Adventure Club

Want to read an exclusive short story with Etan's father Connor and his grandfather Evan, from the time between Book One, *Dreaming the Storm,* and *Into the Storm*?

Want more fiction from Kari, including stories, discounts, and box sets not available anywhere else? Want to hear about locations, research, and other cool things that inspired this story and beyond? All that and adorable pet photos, too?

Join The Confidential Adventure Club and get a thank you gift of *In the Eye of the Storm*, an exclusive short story from The Storms of Future Past Series, and a whole lot more at www.smarturl.it/sofp-welcome.

Hope to see you there!

Novels:

Until Death

The Dream Thief

Dreaming the Storm: Book One of the Storms of Future Past Series

Joining the Storm: Book Two of the Storms of Future Past Series

Fighting the Storm: Book Four of the Storms of Future Past Series

Novellas:

Songs in the Mountain

Legacy of the Land

Restricted Species

The Becalmed

In the Pines

Short Stories:

Renovations

Intentions

The Garbage Belt

The Seeds of Love

Wicked Bone

The Sound of Murder

Terminalia

Little Five: A Terminalia Story

Reflections

Collections:

Fantastic Women: A Dark Fantasy Novella Trio

Fantastic Shorts: Volume 1 - A Fantasy Short Story Collection

"Kari Kilgore is an author to watch—her lyrical voice a siren song; her insight, conjured voodoo."

—Richard Thomas, author of *Breaker* and *Tribulations*

www.ingramcontent.com/pod-product-compliance
Lightning Source LLC
Chambersburg PA
CBHW032038180726
48284CB00008B/2640